So Not a White Knight

A 1Night Stand Story

By
Starla Kaye

Copyright © 2016 by Starla Kaye
ISBN: 978-1-68361-059-5
Cover art by Tibbs Designs

Published by
Decadent Publishing Company, LLC

Look for us online at:
www.decadentpublishing.com

~A Note from the Author~

I'm a dreamer, a lover of happy endings, and especially of that fabled "white knight" who rides in to save a woman. Okay, in reality I'm a very independent, can take care of myself woman. I don't need a man to save me. But, oh, in my heart of hearts, the idea seems so nice. And I'm married to a man who is my personal "white knight."

I've written many romances, with all kinds of heroes: medieval knights, modern day and historical cowboys, pirates, Regency lords, commanders of spaceships, and lots of businessmen. In each story the hero struggles with the heroine who is perfect for him. He butts heads with the woman for so many different reasons. He can't resist her, and then fights with himself about the attraction that he believes weakens him in some way. Or he lets the outside world get in the way of his romantic relationship.

In So Not a White Knight, my hero is a businessman blinded by ambition and what the outside world requires of his success. He loses the romantic man he once was, and he loses the woman meant for him. Through a twist of fate and a stroke of luck, he is given a chance to redeem himself with her. He is gifted with an opportunity to be the man of her dreams...and, hopefully, of her future.

I love to hear from readers and you can contact me at starla@starlakaye.com .

Dedication

To all those women who dream and dare to take a chance on their dream

Chapter One

"Well, damn," Shane said in an appreciative drawl. "What got into you, sweet thing?"

Essie Reynolds beamed at his compliment. When the extremely hot cowboy ambled up behind his wife, she stopped Skyping with her friend Kendra. Essie had just stood up from her desk chair in her home office to do a little model's spin. On a whim, this last Saturday in August she wanted a complete change in her appearance. She'd grown tired of conforming to what was expected of her, in all parts of her life. She wanted to begin the "new her," and this was her first test for reactions.

Kendra blinked without saying a word. Essie worried about having gone too far, too soon. Except Shane didn't seem to think so, which was encouraging. She wanted a man to see her as more than a brainiac with no particular appeal. She wanted to be memorable.

"So you approve of the new haircut, the different clothes?" Essie asked.

Earlier today, she'd shown her regular

hairdresser a photo from the Internet and announced she wanted to cut off her shoulder-length hair and try the short, flirty style. The woman frowned and tried to change her mind. The beautician also resisted changing what Essie considered a mousy-brown color to something more vibrant, almost black. "I'm not sure about the color with your skin," she'd protested. But Essie held firm to her decision.

"Hell yes," he said, still sounding admiring.

She ran her hand over the sleek bangs almost hiding her left eye. Never before had she worn bangs. Her mother disliked the look. Until now, she'd pretty much gone along with her mother's decisions for her. This little rebellion was new and fun. Although, when she went to her parents' home tomorrow for the family's regular Sunday lunch, she didn't expect a good experience. They would not be pleased at all with the changes. Their problem. They would have to adjust.

Carson moved behind Kendra and Shane, grinning. He held a wiggling six-month-old baby in his strong arms. "Ditto, definitely."

"She's so precious," Essie said, sitting down again and feeling more than a bit envious. She wanted what her three friends shared, some day. A man who loved her and a baby to cuddle. Only rarely had one of her parents hugged her. She couldn't remember them cuddling her older brother or sister, either. They weren't warm-and-fuzzy people, something she'd accepted long ago.

Kendra frowned at her cowboys. "How about you two giving me some alone time with Essie? Go play with our daughter. Better yet, get the munchkin bathed and dressed for bed."

Shane winked at Essie. "Leather looks good on you. So does that sexy-as-hell short cut." He fingered Kendra's long hair. "But I don't want this beautiful mane cut off."

Carson tried to hold his daughter closer to his chest, but she had none of it. She arched backward and reached out her pudgy arms toward her mother. He twisted away so Kendra was out of reach. "Guess it's time for bath playtime. Meaning I'll end up almost as wet as Evie will. The kid loves to splash."

He smiled and winked just as Shane had done. "Tell Kendra where you got those skintight leather pants. I'm buying her a pair right away."

Kendra blew out a breath of irritation, making Essie laugh. "I thought you liked my tight jeans."

"Oh, darlin', we sure do," Shane and Carson confirmed at the same time.

"Still...." Shane added with a sexy grin.

Evie squirmed for all she was worth, snagging her fathers' attention. Shane pulled her from Carson's arms and then the men walked off.

"I want *that*," Essie said on a sigh.

"What? An ornery baby like Evie?" Kendra asked, smiling with pride.

"Someday, yes." Essie watched the men disappear from the kitchen where her friend sat at the table in a bay window. "What I meant, though, is sex-in-boots, like your cowboys."

Kendra chuckled. "Cowboys aren't your type. But, yeah, they are darn sexy. Mine, all mine." Her eyes sparkled with pleasure.

Essie felt a stronger twinge of envy, but her friend was right. Other than Shane and Carson, cowboys didn't appeal to her. She preferred

3

businessmen. Something about a suit on a man did it for her. Lately, the men she'd dated, even those in well-tailored suits, left her cold. So maybe a cowboy....

"I want a stud muffin. A man who can show me some serious fire in bed," she admitted, trying not to remember the last time a man brought her close to an orgasm. She took care of that on her own, after the man left, or after she went home. But she dreamed of it.

Kendra gaped at her. "Stud muffin? Fire in bed?"

She puffed up with indignation. "I'm tired of men who don't have even a hint of a wild side. Missionary sex done at record speed—"

"Whoa! What have you done with my ultra-conservative, easily embarrassed friend?" Kendra hesitated, her brow pinched in curiosity. "We've never talked about S E X before."

Essie snorted. "Well, it's personal stuff. But I'm frustrated, way beyond it."

Once more, she thought back to the man she'd dated the last couple of years, and the one before him. Her father had thrown both men at her, trying to guide her to the "right" possible husband. Neither were "keepers," in her opinion. Although Trevon seemed to have potential...until he didn't. She'd tolerated Daniel for too long and ended things with the lawyer last week. Tomorrow, she planned to tell her parents to back off. From now on, she would find men who actually suited her. That conversation wouldn't be pleasant.

She glanced at the photo of her parents on the corner of her desk. They matched in attitude and favored expensive, conservative clothing. Nothing wrong with that, except...it was boring. Besides, they didn't look happy or in love with each other. She wanted more than what they had in a marriage. Respecting each other enough to let the other person go their own way most of the time—other than social appearances they made together—wasn't what she wanted. She'd already seen a hint of that kind of relationship when seeing Trevon Chanders.

"I'm feeling rebellious." How out of character for her. For thirty-five years, she'd tolerated her parents almost running her life, even going into chemical engineering at her father's guidance. She was good at it, but she didn't love her work. She tolerated it.

Kendra cocked an eyebrow. "I see. This has to do with your family, doesn't it?"

Essie nodded. "They're good people, just so blasted conventional in every way. Until now, I've emulated them. But I've come to realize I don't want to do it for the rest of my life."

"Good for you." Kendra smiled in approval.

"I've spent a lot of years doing what they wanted of me, going places they approved of. I can't tell you how many mind-numbing symphonies I've attended, how many operas, how many art openings. Not bad things to do, just not what draws me."

"Wow. You've been doing a lot of serious thinking, haven't you?"

"Yes." On her birthday a couple of months ago, she'd realized how unhappy she was with her life, with the men she dated, and with what her parents expected of her. And even more with her job as the lead chemist in her father's Houston-based oil company.

"I'm ready for some changes, none of which my

family is going to approve of. That's a given."

Kendra studied her. "Like the haircut, which I do like. Like the leather pants, which my men like." She hesitated. "And this sudden desire for a stud muffin."

"All of it. I'm beginning to have a real nesting desire. First, though, I want something magical to remember the rest of my life." She sighed. "I want one night with a sexy beast."

"*Sexy beast*," Kendra repeated, grinning. "Why for only one night?"

From her limited experience with men, they were all "hot and wild" but only for a disappointing amount of time. Then life outside the bedroom got in the way. "Because I'm practical, honest with myself. A sexually demanding man is a rarity in this world. But maybe I can find one good for at least a night, maybe two. I'm determined to give it try."

"I live with two super-sexual men," Kendra stated, with a dreamy look. "Let me tell you, I couldn't be happier. Although, sometimes, they wear me out." She giggled. "Bless them."

"Count yourself lucky," Essie said, again envious. "Besides, I'm not sure I have the kind of stamina you do." She might, but she'd never found the opportunity to find out and didn't think she ever would. "Which is why I'll eventually look for a man more familiar to me. A businessman, a less boring one than those I've dated so far."

Kendra shook her head, looking sad. "I hope you don't just settle for someone who can't make you happy."

It was up to *her* to make herself happy. But she did want to be with someone she could share a life with, be content. "Before I go the comfortable route, I want to detour down a wilder path. For one night, or one weekend." She blew out a frustrated breath, and her new bangs fluttered around. "That's why I called you today. Because I don't know where to find a highly sexual man, willing to settle for one night of giving me mind-blowing orgasm after orgasm. Please me, not just him." The key element. None of her men so far took longer than necessary for themselves. As if "mutual satisfaction" was an unknown concept to them.

Kendra's eyes widened at Essie's blunt declaration. "You think *I* know of such a man? Well, besides my cowboys."

"Can you hook me up with the matchmaker you went through? Madame Evangeline, wasn't it?" Essie looked with pleading at her friend. "She managed to give you what you wanted. Actually, more than you asked for." Twice as much. But Essie knew that would be way more than what she could handle. One gifted man for one wonderful night couldn't be asking too much.

Kendra gushed out, "Absolutely! She's a bit pricy, but you can afford her services." She looked thoughtful. "Let me find her information, and I'll get back with you."

"Soon, okay? You can't imagine how much I need this little adventure."

***

Trevon sat in the great room of the log cabin outside of Oklahoma City. He looked out the large window at the forested acreage. His thoughts turned inward; frustrations in so many parts of his life left him on edge. Because of his mood, his partner in the Houston architectural firm had insisted he leave for a while, at least for the weekend. So, he'd come here to his place of solace from his hectic business life. And his disappointing personal life, too.

As the front man representing the firm, he attended far too many social functions. Four years ago when they'd decided to grow the firm to something in demand, Trevon sacrificed more than he should have. Newly married, Ed's concentration was torn between the company and his new wife. He had managed to handle both well. Not Trevon. He had let the public relations demands become his focus and failed to maintain his relationship with Essie Reynolds. He'd regretted her walking away from him every day since then. Maybe they wouldn't be together now, but maybe they would be.

He blew out a breath, disgusted with his current situation. He'd been in an arrangement with three women for the last few years, almost since Essie left. The firm's reputation, his financial success, his charisma all worked to make him a much sought after bachelor in the Houston area. Women wanted to be seen with him, wanted to go to his bed. In an attempt to control that, he'd found several women with similar problems. Their reputations required them to be in the public eye, needing someone suitable on their arm, someone not interested in tying them down. And they were all sexual by nature. They served each other's desires of the moment, whatever they were. He usually spent a weekend with one or another of them. They were aware of each other and didn't mind. They weren't exclusive with him, either.

He was supposed to have flown with Sabrina in

her personal jet to a resort in Cabo this weekend, but his enthusiasm had waned. Before leaving Houston, he'd told her about changing his mind. She hadn't sounded disappointed. She would find someone else to go with her. Her basic lack of concern should bother him, except it didn't. Their relationship wasn't important to either of them.

He thrummed with longing to spend some intense hours loving a woman. These women were using him far more than he did them. He'd become on-call for when they wanted sex. But sex with each of them had become boring. It was more about how quickly they could reach the point of explosion and then go their separate ways.

He couldn't remember the last time any of his women spent time just talking with him, even arguing with him. He'd appreciated Essie's quick mind, her sharp intellect, and spent many evenings engaged in discussions on this or that. Until he had gotten too busy for them, and for her.

Why think so much about her? Maybe because he'd seen her a week ago with the lawyer she was now involved with. Daniel Brantley, if he remembered right. The man left her alone a number of times while going off to network with someone else. She'd looked so...lonely, but accepting. Dammit, she deserved better treatment!

Ass that he'd been, he hadn't treated her any better. Hindsight. If you knew something you could have done differently.... But you didn't get do-overs in life.

He got up from his favorite leather chair and began pacing around the room. To his annoyance, he sported a killer erection. However, he refused to call any of his women. They weren't who he wanted. And *who* he wanted didn't want him anymore.

He stopped in front of the window, puzzling over the problem. *Jackson Castillo.* He hadn't talked with his friend in months. Jackson was involved with some woman who liked playing matchmaker to clients in need of help meeting someone new. From what he remembered, she arranged short arrangements for people she accepted as clients.

A one-night stand might be exactly what he needed to get him out of this funk of the moment. He didn't want to put himself out in the Houston dating scene again and be approached by a swarm of women—as before his current arrangement—who wanted the multi-millionaire bachelor and not the man behind that image.

Okay, what was her name? Jackson called her Madame something.

He pulled his cellphone from his jeans pocket and called Jackson. Hopefully, he would answer and be able to help him get connected with the matchmaker.

Yet his gut churned. Did he really want to do this? No. But, again, he'd blown his chance at the woman he couldn't forget.

***

Essie drew in a steadying breath, standing on the front porch of her parents' massive Colonial-style house with all its elegance and manicured lawns, a showcase house designed to impress people, a place to hold extravagant parties for Houston's elite. It wasn't a "home," and it didn't make her comfortable.

These every-Sunday brunches with their strained atmosphere were not something she looked forward to. Particularly this one.

Get it together. Be confident. You can do this.

Good thoughts, but she was still anxious about seeing her family today...revealing her new look. She all but shook in the high-heeled boots, looking in concern down at the pants she wore. Most of the time she chose a traditional dress—simple, tasteful—to these get-togethers. She had bought several new dresses yesterday, too. Tighter, with lower necklines to reveal some cleavage. She'd decided to save those for another time. Besides, she felt comfortable in these tight, black leather pants.

Do it. Just ring the doorbell and get on with it.

She tugged her slim shoulder bag up once more and pushed her thumb on the doorbell button. A symphonic-sounding ring echoed through the house. Breathing deep again, she waited for someone in her family to answer the door.

She'd parked in the circle drive behind Monty's sleek black Corvette and Samantha's Lexus SUV. Everyone was here. Good. It would be better to confront her parents and older brother and sister at one time. Better, not necessarily easier, although she didn't expect more than surprised looks from her siblings. They would not be her problem.

Her sister's significant other, Harrison Wadsworth, pulled open the oversized door. His eyes widened, and he blinked in surprise, then he smiled and his eyes twinkled.

Tipping her chin up, she said, "It's *not* funny."

He shook his head, still smiling. "You're right, it's not amusing. Startling, for sure. You have to know that."

She did, which was part of why her stomach fluttered with nerves.

"My amusement had to do with thinking about how Thomas and Amanda will react." He chuckled. "I almost begged out of this today, but now I'm glad I came. This will prove to be interesting."

"A huge understatement, I'm sure." She stepped around him into the Italian marble foyer. The floor sparkled like glass. "I suppose the others are already at the dining table, waiting for me."

He closed the door and moved beside her. "I've got your back, Essie." He took her purse and set it on the antique, ornate hall tree, where she always placed it when visiting here. Her sister's purse already sat there.

His comment and implied support meant a lot. But it was up to her to follow through with revealing her new look, as well as her decision to finally be more aggressive, more in charge of what she chose to do and where she went. And with *whom*.

Still, it was reassuring to walk with her sister's handsome partner in business and in life. Her parents hadn't been overjoyed when they first met him. Despite his former reputation as something of a playboy in Houston, Samantha and Harrison had been together almost two years. He—actually, both of them—didn't want to go the marriage route. It had taken time for her parents to accept their decision.

If her year-older sister could stand up for herself and do what she wanted, Essie could, too.

They walked together in silence to the formal dining room where the others waited. She was about ten minutes late for the meal always scheduled for exactly one o'clock on Sundays. If she hadn't almost changed her mind about coming and sat in her car outside her condo, telling herself to be an adult about facing her parents, she would have been on time.

Harrison inched back and let her step into the room first. Her stomach knotting in discomfort, she went to her usual seat next to her brother, on her father's left side. Like Harrison, Monty gaped at her and then gave a hint of a smile.

"What have you done?" her mother asked in a distressed voice from the other end of the table. "Your hair." She swept her gaze up and down Essie's new clothes. "That...that outfit." Her tone grew louder with each word.

Essie fought not to reach up and touch her short locks, or to squirm under the steady appraisal. "I'm trying something...more interesting...more me." All right, even she was still adjusting to her changes.

"Are you having some kind of midlife crisis?" her father accused, his eyes narrowed.

Harrison stepped behind her and then pulled out her chair. As she sat and he helped her move closer to the table, he leaned down to whisper in her ear, "Be strong."

She hadn't grasped how everyone, including her parents, must have seen her as unwilling to stand up for herself. Why had she acted so unassertive for all these years? Because she picked her battles and hadn't found a worthy one until now.

She picked up the linen napkin beside her plate and carefully placed it over her lap, thinking about her siblings. Unlike her brother and sister, she'd allowed her parents to mold her. Samantha had gone off to college and returned to Houston but declined a position with their father's oil company. Having always intended for all of his grown children to work there, he'd tried to change her mind. Samantha held her own and went to work for Harrison's successful tourist business instead, where she was currently a full partner.

Monty, like Essie, did work for the family oil company, but by *his* choice, as CFO. Once, he'd been manipulated by their parents. They'd convinced him to date and soon after to marry the daughter of one of their father's longtime friends. Their divorce a couple of years later frustrated both families. He still worked for the company, but he didn't allow them control over his personal life anymore.

She smoothed her hands over the napkin, digging up her courage, and looked straight at her father. "This isn't a midlife crisis. I'm too young for that." She refused to look away from his annoyed expression. "I simply wanted to make some changes. It's long past time I did so."

"Some *drastic* changes," her mother challenged. Her perfectly made-up face pinched in irritation.

Her sister intervened. "I like it. The haircut, even the darker color. It looks nice on you." Her eyes twinkled. "And I must say those pants—"

"Look ridiculous," her father blustered, commanding attention again.

Essie fisted her hands in her lap, considered getting up and leaving. But her brother reached over under the table and squeezed her knee in sympathy, encouragement. He leaned closer and said quietly, "I'm proud of you for doing this."

Her father scowled at him, but Monty squeezed her knee a final time and straightened in his chair.

"Are we to expect *more* changes? More inappropriate clothing?" He reached for the platter of sliced roast beef in front of him, passing it to her sister.

Essie watched Samantha take the platter and fork some of the delicious-smelling meat onto her plate. She noted gentle understanding on Harrison's face, the exasperation on her mother's. She tipped out her chin and said, "Yes."

Her father's expression tightened, as if waiting for more of an explanation. He wouldn't like any of it. Yet she knew that it was time to tell them about breaking up with their latest chosen man for her, someone they approved of who would fit into *their* social world. A nice, decent man. A respected Houston attorney with political ambitions. Nice, but oh so boring.

"I've decided to express myself *my* way. My new wardrobe is only one of the changes I've made." *Just tell them.* "Daniel and I are no longer seeing each other."

"*What?*" her father snapped, his gaze revealing incredulity.

"Since when?" her mother added, bristling. "If you had an argument of some kind, I'm sure—"

"We didn't argue. I realized we weren't right for each other and would never be. *I* ended the relationship." The second one she'd ended. The first one having been harder. Unlike Trevon, though, who hadn't tried to convince her to stay with him, Daniel hadn't taken the breakup, the hit to his ego, well. He offered her a week or so to come to her senses. She'd told him she had. The jerk left her sitting alone in the middle of their favorite restaurant.

Her father shook his head, grumbling, "I'll have a

talk with him. We'll work this out."

"You should stay out of this," Samantha inserted, pinning him with a stern look. "We all love you and Mother, but you can't control our lives."

"Certainly not yours," he declared, frowning at Harrison.

Harrison looked him in the eye and said, "It's been the best decision either of us has made."

An uncomfortable silence reigned for a couple of minutes.

Monty focused on his father, body tense. "You're going to have to accept what makes Essie happy, whatever changes she chooses to make." He didn't back down at his father's frown known to bring most people in line with his way of thinking. "Or you might lose her."

For the first time Essie could remember, the hardness left her father's expression, concern replacing it. Both of her parents loved her, in their own far-from-emotional way. And she loved them as well, but she couldn't remain under their control.

"I'll be all right, Dad. So will you and Mom." It had been a long time since she'd referred to them as anything but the more formal Mother and Father.

It took him a second before he sighed and nodded. "I'll try, but...." But it would be hard went unsaid but understood.

Her mother didn't say a word. Her brow furrowed in thought.

Essie looked from one to the other, feeling calmer now, stronger. "Trust me. I'm not going to go crazy on you. I just need to express myself in my way."

Samantha passed the platter of meat to

Harrison. "Well, I'm glad that's all settled. Let's eat. I'm starving and this roast looks wonderful, as always."

Essie knew things were far from settled between her and her parents. Baby steps. She needed to go slow in revealing the changes she still wanted to make. One thing she *wouldn't* be telling them about was her trying to make an arrangement with the matchmaker.

Chapter Two

I am delighted you contacted me after being recommended by Kendra Barlow. Kendra Carter, I mean. It pleased me that her arrangement with the two cowboys worked out for everyone involved. And they have such a beautiful baby girl now, which I'm sure you know. Evie, named after me, I'm told, which means a lot to me.

Essie had snuck away from working on the latest complicated project with the other chemical engineers. She had been checking her email almost constantly since sending a message to Madame Evangeline five days ago. The waiting left her a mess. Many times she'd almost sent an email about changing her mind. It was a relief to have been answered at last. She returned to the message, anticipation threading through her.

I am pleased to tell you I accept you as a client. In fact, I have already begun my search for the type of man you requested. Someone who, apparently, is quite different from the kind of men you have been seeing. This I learned from your friend Kendra. She didn't want me to take the "sexy beast, stud muffin" idea too far. Of course, that was what she got, times two. Still, she worries about you.

Essie sighed. She understood her worry and forgave her good friend for butting in. But she hoped the matchmaker would stay focused on what *she* had requested.

Drawing in a nervous breath, she returned once more to the lengthy message.

She meant well, I'm sure. But I will pursue finding a man such as you requested. Actually, I already have several possible men in mind. I will get back to you in a few days with my recommendation.
Sincerely, Madame Evangeline.

A few days? It was hard to wait any longer, especially with having second thoughts about this kind of arrangement. Okay, second, third, and fourth thoughts. But she would not to back away.

She didn't know whether a response from her was expected, but she wrote one anyway.

Thank you for agreeing to take me on as a client. As you said, Kendra has my best interests at heart. She sees this whole idea as far from my normal behavior. True, but I still wish to do this. I look forward to hearing back from you.
Essie Reynolds.

Her father stepped into her office doorway just as she hit *SEND*, capturing her attention. Her face heated at the idea of him finding out about what she was doing. He would be horrified.

Closing her email, she looked up at him. "Did we have a meeting scheduled I've forgotten?" They didn't run into each other here, unless they had a meeting. She often got so involved in a project she forgot everything else, including meetings.

He shook his head, walking with his usual confidence into the room. Then his glance caught the low-cut neckline of the top she wore beneath the lab coat. He blinked in surprise, even after she'd warned him about making changes. He took a second before he said, "Another new blouse, I see."

"Top, Dad," she corrected him, though it seemed silly. She didn't want to move out from behind her desk because he would surely have a stroke if he saw the skinny jeans she wore. With the kind of work she did, she didn't see the point in wearing dresses anymore, unless she had a meeting.

"Yes, top," he repeated, as if it were a new word he was trying to understand. She suspected the hint of cleavage made him uncomfortable. To his credit, he didn't comment.

"Is there something you wanted?"

He straightened his shoulders beneath the tailored suit coat. His chin appeared set in determination, but she noted a surprising hesitance in his troubled eyes. "I've talked with Daniel. He's calmer now, ready to forgive you—"

Irritation thrumming through her, she cut him off. "You shouldn't have talked with him. My decision stands. We are *not* good together." They never were, not from their first awkward date. They'd just become a habit. One she'd stopped.

Her father's mouth tightened for a second. "Nonsense, Essie. The two of you have a lot in common."

"No, we really don't." Maybe the way they'd been raised, their financial states, and certain social functions. Not enough, in her biased opinion.

"Your mother and I—"

She held up a hand. "I love you both, but it's time you let me handle *my* life."

"I warned you this would be hard for me." He blew out a deep breath, looking torn. "So, no more matchmaking?" He sounded like he still didn't want to back down.

Matchmaking. Her stomach fluttered as she thought about Madame Evangeline's matchmaking attempt for her...at least for one night. She couldn't tell him about that. Ever. It would be embarrassing.

"I can manage my own romantic relationships." Since she didn't run into a lot of unmarried men during her workdays, or any place else, she would have to resort to online matchmaking websites. A depressing idea. Yet, she wanted to have a full life, like Kendra and her cowboys. She longed for a husband and children.

"Okay." He appeared defeated. "Your mother will be harder to convince, though." With a last look at her, he turned and left the office. She knew the powerful owner of a major Texas oil company was sulking. He usually got his way. She collapsed back in her chair, relieved the encounter hadn't gone too badly. *Yeah for me.*

Her thoughts shifted to Kendra again. If she could just have one night of bliss, it would be enough for her. Hopefully. Kendra had gotten that from her arrangement. She'd ended up being in love with the two men she now shared her life with, marrying one of them after ending up pregnant by him from their first time together. The other man she loved almost as much, and the three were happy as a family unit.

Essie wanted to experience wild, abandoned sex for one long night, but she didn't want to end up pregnant from the experience. Protection would be key on both sides. She was on the pill. Maybe she should take along a box of condoms, just to be safe, in case the man failed to bring some.

She jotted a note on her calendar to take care of the matter. A glance at the wall clock told her it was time to get back to work. With no enthusiasm, she got up and walked into the lab. One of these days, she would gather enough courage to quit this job.

***

"I had a few minutes, and thought I would check in with you," Jackson said, sounding both curious and impatient from across the phone line.

Trevon glanced toward the main workroom, where four men, two women, and his partner were gathered around a large blueprint of their biggest project to date. The plans had recently been approved, and news about their achievement circulated around the city.

When Ed looked in his direction, Trevon held out his cellphone. "I need to take this call. I'll be back in a few minutes."

"I didn't mean to interrupt you at work," Jackson apologized. "Like I said, I wanted to see how it was going."

Trevon had a strange feeling about this, worrying a little as he walked into his office and shut the door. He moved behind his large, ebony desk covered with Post-it notes and other scraps of paper he jotted down ideas on to deal with at some point. "This is about Madame Evangeline, isn't it?"

"Yes. Did you get a message from her?"

"She sent me an email a little while ago, but I haven't read it yet." He sat and brought the computer monitor back to life. "I thought maybe she had turned me down."

"Absolutely not, particularly since I recommended you."

Trevon wondered if that was good or bad. "You aren't setting me up for—"

"No, I was concerned about you when we talked about this matter." Jackson sounded sincere. "Why don't you read Madame Evangeline's email first? I'll wait."

Feeling cautious, Trevon went to his email account and located her message. He opened it, "All right, I'm looking at it."

Trevon,

I'm so pleased Jackson sent you to me. Your request is something of a challenge. The description of the woman you are interested in spending time with is quite specific, right down to her appearance. As if this was someone from your past. I finally asked Jackson what he knew about the matter. I have a much better understanding now, but it may take me a few more days to find your match.

Madame Evangeline.

"It looks like she is taking me on." He thought about his description of the woman he envisioned being with on this date. He groaned. *Damn*. Essie again. He must have described her. "She said she talked to you about my request, about the woman. What did you tell her?"

Jackson took a second before he said with caution, "I told her about Essie, about how you know how much you fucked up with her."

"Great." Trevon ran a hand through his hair. "She probably thinks I'll 'fuck up' with another woman, too."

"No. She believes you'll behave better now. And she hurt for you. She has a very tender heart."

Sympathetic, perfect. He didn't want to be pitied. All he wanted in this arrangement was to spend time with a woman who might want to be seduced by a romantic man. He hadn't shown that side of him in a long time...not since when he and Essie had first begun dating. Somewhere along their way together, he got too lost in the other demands in his life. He had ignored the romantic side because it took too long. And with his other women...well, they only wanted wham-bam-thank-you-sir time. Once more he thought about feeling used by them, like he'd become just a personal sex toy to them.

Jackson snorted. "*Personal sex toy*?"

"Hell! Did I say that out loud?" Trevon groaned.

"Sure did." Jackson hesitated. "Most men wouldn't mind."

His hand threaded through his hair once more. "None of my women have said as much, but it's in the way they treat me. Like they can flip my switch and turn me up to fast and furious." Which usually worked.

"Cheese with that whine?"

Jackson's attitude annoyed him. "You're hi-lar-i-ous," he dragged out the word. "Anyway, Madame Evangeline appears to be searching for the woman I requested."

"Yes, she is. She has great instincts," Jackson said, serious as always.

"Do you know something you aren't telling me?"

"Evangeline doesn't confide in me. Sometimes I wish she would, especially when it involves an old friend of mine." He took a second before adding, "I'm as curious as you are about what happens, who she finds for you. Give me a call when you find out."

Before Trevon could respond, Jackson disconnected in his typical abrupt manner.

**

The quiet *ding* of her cellphone alerted Essie to a new email. After eagerly reading a couple dozen unimportant emails already this morning as she hung around her condo, she hesitated to check it out. She didn't want to be disappointed again.

But she couldn't resist. She muted the movie she'd been sort of watching and reached for the phone on the end table beside her. *Please, please, please let this be from Madame Evangeline.*

A glance told her it was. Her heart did a flurry of beats.

Dear Essie,
I have found the perfect man for you. He is flexible on whether this is for one night or the

weekend.

As anticipation curled through her, she studied the rest of the message.

According to Kendra, I know you have been to the Kauai Driftwood Beach Resort before and liked it very much. So that's where I will send you two. Unless you can't manage it, I have made reservations for one of their best condos for next weekend. Let me know if I need to change the date.

Essie closed her eyes and leaned back to contemplate what she'd read so far. Next weekend. Awfully soon. Those heart flutters sped up. Still, the weekend would be good for her schedule. And she did like the resort.

Opening her eyes, she returned to the message.

I have contacted Trevon Chanders, the man I've decided most meets your requirements. He will check his schedule and get back to me later today. But he's fairly certain that will work for him. Could you please shoot me back a response?
Madame Evangeline

Once more Essie sat back and closed her eyes to contemplate the message. Next weekend. The resort she had been to several times and enjoyed. A man believed to suit what she requested. Oh wow! Now it was all so real.

What name had she said? She glanced back at the email. Trevon Chanders.

Of course, there were a number of Essie

Reynolds she'd learned after googling her name. So there might also be many men with that name. Right?

After a second, she blinked her eyes, her heart hammering. No, it couldn't be him. How could this happen?

Trevon Chanders—co-owner of the prestigious architectural firm in Houston—had recently gotten approval for the design of an exclusive gated condo community on the outskirts of the city. The news was all over TV, the radio, and in the newspaper. She'd read every bit of it, listened to each word said. The Houstonian multi-millionaire constantly appeared in the society pages. He traveled with gorgeous socialites, sexy ones. Women so unlike her: a mousy, somewhat introverted chemical engineer. Why would he need the services of a matchmaker?

The self-description bothered her. It wasn't true any longer. She sported a new, flirty short haircut. Her hair color had changed to almost black, far from "mousy." She'd even taken a class about being more confident in yourself, about being more assertive in dealing with the world around you. And she'd already stood up to her parents. *Go me!*

The new her could handle Trevon Chanders.

But maybe this wasn't the man she knew. It could be some nerd by the same name. Of course, she, too, was on the nerdy side. He could be a timid man who convinced Madame Evangeline he wanted a match with a sexy woman. He could have told her he could give the woman a "really good" time. Maybe he would turn out to be as disappointing in bed as Daniel.

Sexy woman? She wanted to be that, at least one time in her life. But could she pull it off? Why not?

What the heck are you thinking? Her rambling thoughts slid to a halt. She knew in her gut that this man *was* her Trevon Chanders. No! He didn't belong to her anymore, not after being apart almost three years. She'd called things off. And he'd let her. She didn't want anything to do with him again. Lie. She wanted.... What?

She wanted one more night with him—sad, but true. Then she would move forward with her plan to find a man for a suitable husband. Which wouldn't be the likes of Trevon.

Decision made, she wrote a response.

That weekend works for me. I look forward to hearing Trevon Chanders has also accepted the date. Essie Reynolds.

Did he even know he was being matched to her? What a bizarre situation. *Karma. Not hardly.*

With renewed determination, she hit *SEND*. Putting aside her laptop, she hurried to her bedroom. She needed something to wear to knock him on his ass. Let him see the new her, the wilder woman. Let him get a taste of the woman he'd let leave who could now hold her own with him in the bedroom.

Hmmm. Maybe she was taking her "revenge" too far. She wasn't experienced with tantric sex or anything the least bit sensual or even mildly kinky. But she could sure read up on all of it? *Research, research, research. Watch out, Mr. Trevon Chanders!*

***

Next weekend? For some reason, Trevon hadn't thought an arrangement could be made this soon. He glanced at the calendar on the computer screen in front of him. As he'd told Madame Evangeline, that particular weekend worked for him.

He looked toward the wall of windows in his office, and his thoughts turned inward. Could he find the romantic in him again? Or would it be a bittersweet experience because he would be thinking of Essie the whole time? Which he needed to stop doing, but couldn't seem to manage.

Decision made, he sent back his response.

I accept. If the woman agrees, I can assure you we will have a mutually enjoyable time.
Trevon Chanders.

He tried to focus on work again; he had so many phone calls to return, so many emails to answer. A daunting list. Yet, as he went from one task to another, he waited in anticipation for the matchmaker's return message.

As he started to shut down his computer to head home, an email popped up from the woman. He steadied his nerves and opened the message.

My dear Trevon,
The wonderful woman I have matched you with has agreed to that date, as well. I will make travel arrangements for you both and let you know the particulars. All you need to do is go to the Kauai Driftwood Beach Resort, meet this woman, and have a good time together. Both of you.

His heart beat faster at the reality of what was happening, both exciting and a bit unnerving. He hoped he could pull this off. Whoever the woman might be, she deserved his best. He never intended to treat another woman as badly as he had treated Essie.

A last look at the email made him see a final statement.

Your date for this special night—or weekend, whatever you two decide —is Essie Reynolds. After some consideration, I believe she is the woman you need time away with. I hope I'm right.

How had the matchmaker managed to find her? Get her involved with this matchmaking craziness? Jackson said he'd mentioned his previous relationship with Essie to the woman. Trevon had been uncertain about that admission, but now.... Now, he owed his friend a bottle of his favorite, very expensive wine. A case of it.

Essie must have agreed to the one-night stand date. Why? She'd hardly given him a hint of a smile the times they'd seen each other since their break-up.

Did he care about her reasoning? No. Getting another chance with the woman stuck in his heart was all that mattered. He would not blow it this time!

Chapter Three

The warm evening breeze carried the salty scent of the ocean a couple of hundred yards away to Trevon. He sat at one of the Driftwood Terrace Restaurant's outside tables, sipping a glass of beer as he waited for Essie to arrive. Relaxing for a while felt damn good.

He'd gone a hundred-plus miles an hour since making the final arrangements with Madame Evangeline in order to get away for these few days. When even more issues with their new project came up yesterday, he'd worried about having to back out. But no way in hell he would he have done that. So, he had scrambled to get everything back on track with the deal. It had all come together only hours before having to get to the airport in Houston this morning.

A weak headache lingered, a result of too much stress and flying for over twelve hours today. It might be around ten o'clock at night here, but his body knew it was 3:00 a.m. his time. No doubt Essie would feel just as exhausted by the time she got to the resort, which should be any time.

He took another chug of the beer, trying to

remember when he'd last drunk one. Somewhere along the line, Scotch on the rocks or a good wine had become his drink of choice. He liked this change of pace. Curious, he wondered if Essie still liked Cabernet Franc. In case she did, he'd bought a bottle at a shop in Lihu´e on his way to the resort.

In the spattering of lights around the grassy area just beyond the restaurant, he watched a pair of wild chickens pursuing each other. The feral chickens were unique to the Hawaiian Islands, this one in particular, and ran freely around the grounds. He found them entertaining, as did the children chasing after them. What would Essie think of them? Would she like this resort? He had been to nice ones on Maui and Oahu, but this was his first time to Kauai. He liked the slower pace, the less touristy feel here. Would she? Of course, they were only going to have tonight and tomorrow together, unless they decided to take advantage of having the condo for Sunday, too. Time would tell, but he liked the idea.

A toddler boy scurried down the sidewalk not far from him. His harried-looking young mother raced after him. Trevon smiled. He liked kids, but he didn't see himself as a family man. He couldn't remember if he and Essie ever talked about children. His recently engaged twin brother and Tanya were chatting about babies. Better his ex-football playing brother than him. Maybe someday, with the right woman. Yet, he supposed, at forty he should be giving it a lot more serious thought.

Essie. She hadn't been far from his thoughts for a while, even more so since making this arrangement. Anticipation passed through him, along with a sense of unease. He wasn't sure what to expect. He he hoped to earn a second chance with her. She wouldn't make this easy for him, but he could face the challenge. He was sure they would end up in bed together, but he planned to do everything different this time...better. He wanted to seduce the hell out of her.

He yawned. What would she expect of this first night together? Some initial breaking-the-ice conversation? Maybe a simple kiss? More? He was tired. He didn't know how much "more" he could handle tonight. But he would give his best shot at whatever she wanted. Otherwise, he would like to sit on their lanai and talk for a bit then get some sleep and let their real time together start in the morning.

Where was she? He had claimed this spot so he could watch the resort grounds and see the entrance, too. As he glanced in the lobby's direction, he spotted a new group of guests who had arrived on the airport shuttle and were lining up to check in. He sat up straighter and studied the various women in the group. A silver-haired senior with a weary-looking older man. A pair of blonde, peppy, cheerleader types. Then a dark-haired woman in a form-hugging white dress stepped into the line.

His gaze widened, and he switched to full alert mode. Instant attraction. Definitely nice. A man would have to be dead not to appreciate *that. It's not Essie, though.*

He forced down his automatic interest and sipped his beer again. Still, he struggled to pull his gaze away from the hot babe with the short hair.

He sat back and prepared to wait some more. He watched for a woman with shoulder-length brown hair, black-rimmed glasses, and probably wearing nice traveling slacks or maybe a modest dress. Something conservative, like Essie.

Maybe she was still on the shuttle bus.

***

The back of Essie's neck tingled, as if someone stared at her. She had gotten quite a few looks during the long flight and in the four airports today. Some approving, some interested, and some heated. Her face flamed at the reactions, having never experienced anything like this before. Whenever she traveled—which wasn't all that often—she never tried to draw attention to herself. *Blend in* had been her mantra for so long.

Clearly, an updated hairstyle along with more vibrant coloring, having a professional cosmetologist help with her makeup, more than a few hours spent this past week at the gym sweating bullets and toning up, and an investment in a sexy white dress were paying off. *Good, right?* Yes, but still unnerving.

She was reluctant to turn away from the friendly older man checking her in and continue with her performance as a remodeled Essie Reynolds. The new her still felt off, like clothes in the wrong size or something. What would Trevon think?

After pulling in a courage-building breath, she accepted the room key and instructions on how to find the unit. The clerk told her Trevon had already checked in. So, where was he? In the condo? In one of the bars or restaurants on the grounds? He could be anywhere. Just thinking of him made her stomach churn with nerves. Why had she agreed to this time with him? He'd already bruised her heart once when he hadn't argued about her leaving him. Why had *he* sought out the matchmaker?

She clutched the room key tighter. Her thoughts turned to Kendra. Her friend's involvement with Madame Evangeline had turned out well. Essie hadn't expected anything like that. She only wanted a taste of the wilder side for once in her life. Not a date with a Mr. Ho-Hum. She'd requested Mr. Sexy Beast.

She'd gotten Trevon Chanders, a known quantity already. Sort of. Since they hadn't been together in three years. They'd crossed paths, but never spoken to each other. So, other than what she'd read about him, she couldn't say she knew the man now. But she would again, soon.

Resigned to follow through with her commitment, she stepped to the side and turned around. She smiled at the young twentyish woman waiting in line nearby. And then stepped farther away at the lusty gaze of the man with the blonde.

Her stomach fluttered. Would Trevon look at her that way? Even vastly changed, she didn't think she came anywhere close to the kind of women who were seen with him these days. If her father hadn't introduced them and pushed them together in the first place, they would never have been a couple. Things were good in the beginning, really good. But then....

"Ms. Reynolds, shall I take your bags to your unit now?" a teenaged bellhop asked loud enough to be heard over the music drifting from a bar across the lobby. "Or we can deliver them later."

As she glanced at the younger man, she caught sight of a breath-stealing man in the outside eating area of a restaurant not thirty feet away. *Trevon.* He looked intently in her direction, making her nervous. He wore a blue chambray shirt, sleeves rolled up to reveal his forearms. Even from this short distance, she could see a cocky attitude in his expression. Something like both Shane and Carter sported at different times. Cowboy attitude. A wide-brimmed hat sat crown down on the table next to his bottle of beer. She'd never seen him dressed this way.

"Ms. Reynolds?" the bellhop tried again.

She blinked back to the moment. "I—"

Before she could finish the thought, Trevon stood and faced her. Tall, broad shouldered, even better looking than she remembered him. Their gazes locked. One of his thick, dark eyebrows quirked up in question. Then a corner of his mouth lifted in a sexy grin. *Oh, Lord help me.*

"Ma'am?" the bellhop prodded yet again.

Stetson perched with a cocky tilt on his head, Trevon ambled in her direction. Her knees weakened. Warmth curled low inside her. What had she told Kendra she wanted? *Sex-in-boots.* Well, this was exactly that. He had it all—confidence in his stride, long legs covered in worn denim, boots, and oozing testosterone. Her wish come to life...maybe her nightmare.

The charismatic man who drew attention wherever he went—including here—walked up in front of her. Beneath the brim of his hat, a vivid-blue gaze moved ever so slowly over her. He gave her an approving nod and then focused on the bellhop. "I can handle her bags."

Oh, sweet heaven, she'd almost forgotten. Not only was he supremely hot, but also he spoke in his familiar velvety deep voice with a hint of Texas drawl.

A voice that had once whispered naughty things to her in bed. It had made her shiver, all over. Somewhere along the way, he'd stopped doing that.

He pulled out a money clip from the pocket of his jeans and handed the younger man a generous tip. They winked at each other in some kind of male code she didn't want to interpret. She studied his large, tanned hand, recalling what he could do with it...with her. Her nipples tightened into buds. *Perfect! Please don't let him notice.*

When he focused on her once more, his gaze landed precisely there. Her foolish nipples hardened even more, so much they ached.

His eyes turned darker.

They stood there without speaking, taking in each other, for a full minute before someone bumped into one of her suitcases. It fell over and thumped on the tiled floor.

She gasped in surprise and felt her cheeks flaming as she realized how she was ogling him. Hopefully, she hadn't been drooling, too. She might be attracted to him again, but she wasn't quite ready to forgive him for not fighting for her.

"Sorry," apologized the older man she had seen earlier with his silver-haired wife. He leaned down to right the bag.

"Not a problem." Trevon took hold of the handles on the pair of large suitcases. As the other couple walked away, he gave her a teasing grin. "Traveling light?"

Her discomfort grew. "I wanted to be prepared for whatever we ended up doing."

His melting gaze took her in again. "You could have packed a small duffle bag and had more than enough to wear."

The oh-so-wicked promise in those words made her heart skip a beat, two beats, and then race. Could she handle him for a night? Maybe two? She thought about grabbing her bags and running like hell. *Not a chance. Buck up.*

From somewhere inside her, she latched onto a tiny bit of courage to hold her own. "If you brought more than what you're wearing, then *you* over-packed." Had she really said that?

To her relief, he chuckled, amusement dancing in those gorgeous blue eyes. "Ready?"

For him to toss her down on the tiled floor and.... *Yes, yes, yes.* She managed to keep the words in her mouth and instead gave a quick nod. "Where you lead, I will follow."

His wicked, crooked grin flashed again. "Oh, darlin', don't play with fire. Because I can certainly lead you far astray."

"That's what I want," she muttered as he headed off. At least, she thought she did.

He stopped and cocked his head, studying her. "What did you say?"

"Nothing." The chicken side of her made another appearance. She waved him on.

What the hell were you doing back there? Flirting, teasing? Trevon moaned. He trudged down the well-lit winding sidewalk of the main area between the wings of hotel buildings, toward the far building with a few ocean-front condos.

He pulled in a frustrated breath. Awareness and desire tore through him. For Essie, a damn sexy woman in an all-too-revealing hot, white dress walking behind him. He tried not to think about the flirty haircut with the wispy bangs. His fingers ached to smooth them out of the way, see if her hair felt as soft as before.

This woman confused him. Where were those thick dark glasses she used to wear?

God, those eyes. How could he have forgotten how smoky brown they were, how cautious they could be, how inviting, too? And what about her body! She'd been lovely before. Now she was all sexy curves, perfect for a man's hands to wander over. *This* Essie wasn't at all what he'd expected. His Essie had been sweet, almost fragile, and innocent in so many ways. In that dress—*Oh, my God, that dress!*— she was damn spicy. He liked spice!

"Is this some kind of race?" she questioned, sounding winded.

He breathed harder, too, but blamed it on his physical reaction to the little sex-bomb. "Sorry."

Turning toward his destination once more, he bit back a groan. It had been a mistake to look at her again. Those plump breasts struggling inside the low-cut neckline called to him. *Hold me. Squeeze me. Put your mouth on me*. And those legs! Killer long, toned. They used to wrap around him so easily.

Sweat trickled down his back, beaded on his upper lip. He'd missed her, but he hadn't imagined he would react this strong, so quickly. He had made plans for seducing her. Going nice and slow, enjoying every inch of her...of each other. Now, he wanted to thump his chest and go all caveman crazy, make her *his* woman. Already he struggled with a killer erection. Too soon, way too soon.

He felt like an idiot. He needed to downshift, calm everything down. Pulling in a breath, he let go of the suitcases and managed to look her in the eye. "You look good, Essie. The...the changes just surprised me." He thought about how the words sounded wrong and added, "Not that you didn't look nice before."

She arched a thin, dark eyebrow. "A decent save, Trevon, but it could have been better." She smiled. "I know this is awkward, for both of us."

"Clearly," he agreed. "I'll try to get my act together."

She gave a soft laugh and did a little model's spin. "So, the money I spent on this new dress and the new hairstyle were worth it?"

"Oh, honey, definitely," he admitted. He wanted nothing more than to get his hands on the dress, tear it off her. He gripped the suitcase handles tight again.

Her thousand-watt smile ratcheted up another gazillion watts. *Oh damn.*

"How about we get going again?" he choked out, thinking about their short amount of time together and all he wanted to accomplish. His body screamed to him about making the most of every second.

She nodded, and her gaze warmed. Her breaths were deep, making those amazing breasts rise and fall in a way that held his attention. "I'm ready to slip into something...more comfortable...have you do the same," she said in a suggestive whisper.

He sweated some more. "Sounds good to me." He could see them naked and tangled together on the big, over-sized bed in the condo. There were a hundred things he wanted to do.

Trevon went back to pulling the suitcases along, thinking about his goals for their time together. Lost in his thoughts.

"Are you all right?" she asked, walking up next to him. She reached for one of the suitcases. "I can take at least one of these bags."

He tugged the bag out of her reach. "I'm fine. Not at my best. It's been a long day." He tried a reassuring smile. "I apologize."

Her eyes softened. "I understand. It's been a long day for both of us. Let's just get to our place. Get comfortable." She glanced away, her cheeks growing pink, and then met his gaze again. "Maybe later...." She let him figure out what she meant.

What she implied sounded damn good, too, exactly what he wanted. "Yes, later," he agreed, hoping she understood he was all for sliding into bed with her.

The surprising woman winked at him, cheeks still pink. "The clock's ticking."

Chapter Four

*T*he clock's ticking! Essie stood in the middle of the large bathroom in their unit. She'd taken less than a few seconds to tug one of her suitcases away from him and speed in here with it, firmly closing and locking the door. No doubt he still stood in the entryway, wondering what the hell had just happened.

Her heart raced as she took in the impressive room with the polished marble floor, the over-sized walk-in shower meant for more than one person, and the pair of thick, white robes hanging next to the door. What she remembered of the main room itself had been island-style elegance. Beautiful, perfect for lovers. Or maybe that was what her sex-crazed mind envisioned.

Oh, dear Lord, what's happened to me? Sex-crazed? Really?

She drew in a deep, steadying breath, but it didn't help much. She had taunted Trevon about being in a hurry to get it on. Well, not in those exact words, but she'd mentioned getting "comfortable" and added "maybe later." The huskiness in his voice when he'd responded told her he'd put the hints together and approved.

She slumped onto the lowered lid of the toilet, hanging her head. This was all so new to her, this acting bold and brazen. He probably wondered where the brainiac, the woman more comfortable in a chemistry lab than on the social scene, was. He was equally as intelligent, but far more at ease in the public eyes. Their romantic relationship had been comfortable, nothing spectacular. He'd been too distracted by everything going on with the firm he and Ed were building. She'd accepted whatever he gave her without complaint, although she craved more. Finally, she'd decided they would be better separate, and he'd agreed she might be right. That hurt. Still did.

With effort, she put the unpleasant memory aside. She'd surprised him with her new look. His vivid-blue eyes had grown dark, and his nostrils flared as he took her in from head to foot. A couple of times she'd noticed a definite thick ridge in the front of his jeans. His reactions flattered her, making all sorts of tingling sensations sweep through her. She'd missed his reactions and how they made her feel.

So far, her efforts in preparing for this experience were paying off. The money spent on her dress was worth it—his eyes had all but popped out of his head. *Definitely nice!* He'd also kept looking at her hair, appeared to like the change. And the way he'd all but drooled staring at her breasts—much perkier now—made all those hours of working on the weight machines worth the torture.

To be fair, he looked delectable, too. Trevon Chanders in a suit could impress anyone. In jeans, all cowboyed up? She wanted him with every fiber of her being, and that irritated her a whole lot. She didn't want to desire him this much, so soon. In their past, sex hadn't been be-still-my-beating-heart intense. More like just okay. She wanted far more this time. And she'd studied up for the adventure, spending hours devouring several books to increase her knowledge base about sex. She planned to use what she'd learned.

A soft knock on the door snared her attention. "Are you all right?"

He sounded worried, which made her feel ridiculous for having fled from him and hidden away in here.

"I-I'm changing clothes, like I said. Into something more comfortable." Was this the right suitcase? Well, whatever clothing this one held would have to do.

"You don't want to get a glass of wine first. Maybe sit out on the lanai and enjoy the night view of the ocean, talk a little?" He still sounded concerned.

She laid the suitcase on its side and opened it, frowning. "Wine sounds good. Red, I hope."

"I have a bottle of Cabernet Franc, if you still like that." He hesitated. "You're sure you're okay?"

"Yes. Yes, I'm fine. Just give me a few minutes." He remembered her favorite wine. How touching.

As she stared into the wrong suitcase, she huffed in annoyance. If she attempted to exchange this bag for the other one, she might lose her courage. Fine. She would make do with something from the clothes she had brought with her in case she spent Sunday here alone, her "comfort" clothes. Maybe she could just act sexy. Yeah, right. Like she knew how to do that. Whatever. Later she could change into one of the hot little numbers she had picked out to bring him to his knees.

Trevon didn't know what to think. He stared at the closed bathroom door for another few seconds. Had he done something to scare her? He couldn't imagine what it could have been. Unless she'd noticed the erection pressing at the front of his jeans. Did it worry her? She'd seen him aroused before.

He went to the small kitchen for the wine and a pair of glasses. What was she changing into? She wasn't a Victoria's Secret kind of woman. Her lingerie tended to be pretty, just nothing man-killer sexy. He'd never cared. Stripping her down to get at the luscious body beneath whatever she wore had never been a problem. Exactly what he wanted to do now.

Except he wouldn't. He needed to slow the hell down. Should he be changing clothes, too? Into what? He'd already set aside his hat, kicked off his boots. He figured that was enough.

He pulled the wine from the refrigerator to let it warm up slightly. As he carried it to the bar between the kitchen and main room to set it by the glasses, he began counting to a hundred. Patience. Somehow he could muster up some.

At the sound of the bathroom door opening, he looked that way. His breath hitched. *Holy hell!*

Essie took a step from the bedroom and stopped. She stood there, worrying one side of her tempting pink mouth. He remembered the nervous habit of hers, still thought it charming.

"I, uh, picked the wrong bag for my grand exit

into the bathroom." Both embarrassment and annoyance filled her face.

He imagined the other bag held whatever she'd intended to wear for him. Something sexy? He could only hope. Yet he wasn't disappointed at the moment. Those long, creamy legs captured his attention beneath a pair of running shorts barely covering her sweet ass. His pulse picked up speed.

His gaze shifted higher to a good swath of stomach revealed below a cropped sweatshirt top, sleeves cut away. A faded picture of a redheaded mermaid emblazoned over the impressive breasts he so enjoyed, planned to enjoy again...a lot. And her feet were bare, small pink-painted toes drawing his focus back down again.

"Not what you expected, huh?" she asked in clear frustration. She started toward the other suitcase sitting by the front door. "Give me a few more minutes and—"

"No. You look fine," he protested, making her freeze and blink at him in surprise. "Frankly, *that's* pretty darn sexy."

Brown eyes turned smoky, and a smile slid into place. "I could change." Instead, she looked to the wine bucket and glasses next to it. "I know it's getting late and you're probably as tired as I am, but a drink sure sounds good."

His gaze slipped behind her to the bedroom, straight to the king-sized bed. Late or not, he felt energized, ready to shift gears and—

Slow it down.

Trevon pulled in a calming breath. "Lanai?" he questioned, hearing the husky tone in his voice, the near desperation. He reached to pick up the wine. He needed his hands on something because he really wanted them to be on her sweet body.

She padded over on bare feet and snagged the glasses. "Lanai works for me. I love sitting outside at night here, listening to the waves roll onto the beach."

He let her lead the way to the sliding glass doors, admiring the sway of rounded hips, an ass he ached to touch. For a chemical engineer, she had one damn sexy body. If all went where he planned it would, he intended to know every inch of her again before they left this Hawaiian paradise.

She flipped on the dim light for the lanai on her way outside. It gave a romantic feel to the moment, an intimacy he liked. Beyond them, whispery clouds drifted around the dark sky, revealing a bare handful of stars. The air was humid, but not as thick as earlier in the day. A fishy scent drifted on the gentle breeze.

Trevon took a second to inhale deep. Essie's familiar scent always did it for him. Something soft and feminine, flowery, but not strong. He wanted to move behind her, nestle his head to her nape, and draw in more of the enticing smell. He longed to nibble at her neck. His hands ached to reach around and hold each of those fleshy breasts beneath the sweatshirt top. Lord, his troubles grew by the moment.

Oblivious to her effect on him, she stopped outside for a second and seemed to take in the night. Then she moved to set the glasses on the round patio table in the center of the space. That done, she went to stand against the wrought-iron railing to gaze toward the Pacific Ocean a couple of hundred yards away. She looked even more tempting. But then every move she made, every glance she spared him lured him more and more.

"Have you ever been here before?" she asked without turning around. "Kauai? Or this resort?" The breeze fluttered the short ends of her hair.

He wanted to glide his fingers through that hair. He had always preferred long hair, until now. The erection pressing at his jeans became hard to ignore. She was just so damn irresistible.

To distract his body, keep him from doing something neither of them was ready for, he went about the task of pouring them each a glass of wine.

"Neither one," he answered, as he remembered she had asked him a question. He stepped next to her, and handed her a glass. "Oahu many times on business. The big island, too. But I've been thinking about getting a vacation condo on Maui."

She faced him, her eyes brightening. "I would love to do something like that, but...." Some of the pleasure in her gaze disappeared.

"But?" he prodded, missing the eagerness he'd seen.

She turned away and took a sip of wine before explaining. "I don't get away from my work very often. Unless it's to a conference of some kind." She shifted, seeming uneasy. "My life is pretty dull, which you might remember. I'm fairly boring."

He knew all of her family—her father, active on many important boards around Houston; her mother, Amanda, owner of an exclusive interior design firm and involved all over the community; her brother, Montgomery, CFO of the family oil company; and her sister, Samantha, partner in an exclusive tour business. They were all over the social news, unlike Essie, who never liked the limelight. But he had never thought of her as "boring."

"For the most part mine is, too." At least his life beyond his duties to represent the company. His personal life was far different from what the world saw of him. Not even his current lady "friends" knew the man behind his public persona.

She angled her head, and her eyes flashed in challenge. "You're in the papers all the time. If there is a major social event, you're there." Irritation slid into place, and she looked to the ocean again. "With a beautiful woman hanging on your arm."

He winced. "It's good for business, which I'm sure you understand. You grew up in an important Houstonian family," he countered in defense. He was trying to get his partner to step up for some of it, but the change took time. "I can't deny I escort some beautiful women to those events." His three lovers by arrangement, but she may not have realized that.

She gave an unladylike snort.

His women, his lifestyle...both were sore subjects between him, his twin brother, and his father. He wasn't as "wild" as they believed. Recently, he'd become ready to rein in certain aspects of his life, although his family didn't know yet. They would just hound him about it even more.

"Why did you decide to try Madame Evangeline's services?" he asked to change the subject. "This doesn't seem like something you would do."

She shifted around and leaned back against the railing, appearing to weigh her response, studying him. "How about you go first?"

The way her breasts thrust toward him made him lose the thread of conversation. "What?"

"You explain first," she repeated, puzzled.

He frowned, still a bit embarrassed by having approached the elite matchmaker. "You won't believe me, but I wanted…." Did he really want to admit his actual reason?

Her expression softened, and she said with gentleness, "You don't have to tell me. I'm just curious."

He hesitated, considering what to say, and decided to be honest. "I wanted something different from my normal experiences."

"Meaning?" She sipped her wine, those warm-brown eyes encouraging.

He turned to glance toward the ocean, uncomfortable with what would sound ridiculous. "I wanted a chance to seduce a woman. Take my time with her." He sighed. "That's not what my sexual relationships are like these days. They're all about rushing, getting the deed done. And I realize how harsh it t sounds." He shrugged. "It's the truth, though."

"Sad," she murmured.

He heard in what she didn't say—that was what she remembered of their relationship, too. At least in the end. God, it made him feel worse.

"I wanted a chance to find the romantic in me again." He faced her, and the sadness in her eyes tore at him. "Essie, I know it's still there."

She shrugged, in disbelief, maybe in challenge. "Want to know what I originally requested?"

He nodded, more than curious.

"I requested a 'sexy beast' to give me one night of orgasm after orgasm, a memory of a lifetime." She made the admission with a jut out of her chin, a hint of daring.

He blinked at her. She'd never pushed in bed, seemed satisfied with anything. He must have missed some major signals. *Idiot*.

He took a long swallow of wine. He hated the idea of her being with some other man acting the "sexy beast." He'd tried hard not to ever think of her being with another man. "Why did you decide to accept this date with me?" he asked quietly, nervous about her answer.

She took several seconds before answering. "Curiosity. I'd thought I wanted some kind of payback from you for how we ended. But I was wrong about that." She lowered her gaze. "We wanted different things back then. Maybe me, more than you. In a relationship, I mean. "

Her bluntness touched him. He'd been an ass to let her walk away from him. They should have talked it over. He shouldn't have just let their struggling relationship stop so easily. She deserved his reasoning about his choice to be here. "I wanted another chance to be with you." He didn't add he wanted much more than that.

"Really?" Something like hope flittered in her eyes, vulnerability.

"Yes."

He set his glass on the table, took hers and set it down as well. Stepping in front of her, stocking-covered feet to bare toes, he reached out to cup the side of her face with his right hand. She sucked in a nervous breath. With a reassuring smile, he smoothed his thumb over her lips, making her tremble. Her response left him aching, but he wouldn't push her. Not yet.

"Just give me a chance, Essie." When one of her eyebrows lifted and her breath hitched, he held his thumb over her lips to keep her from speaking. "Please."

To his surprise, she inched out her small tongue and licked his thumb.

His heart skipped several beats, and his gut tightened. "Whoa, baby. Don't play with fire so soon." He drew in a deep, settling breath. "Be patient with me."

As he dropped his hand, she grinned, a hint of playfulness in those expressive eyes. "I'm a chemical engineer who works on endless new formulas. Patience is my second nature." She lifted a hand to stroke the stubble on his chin. "But, in this situation, I can't wait for long."

Blood pulsed to the wrong spot, making his erection even harder. Making it difficult to think. He fought hard not to drag her into his arms and abandon his plan.

"Maybe we should go to bed now...I mean to sleep. We...we're both exhausted. Right?" He looked past her toward the main room, thought about the big bed. "Maybe we should sleep in separate places tonight. The sofa makes into a bed. I can sleep there." *Say no. God, please say no.*

To his regret, she nodded and picked up the glasses, heading for the sliding doors. "That might be a good idea."

No, it isn't. He ached to take the suggestion back. *Give the lady time.* He doubted he would sleep a wink, thinking about Essie in bed all alone, wanting to be there with her.

Chapter Five

Movement on the bed jarred Essie from deep sleep. As if drawn to the heat beside her, she turned to her side and snuggled close to the warmth. Her brain couldn't seem to connect the dots, but something was off about the situation.

Still, she inched closer without fully waking, nor wanting to. Her arm snaked over a very naked, very masculine body. At the touch of skin not as soft as hers, at the feel of wiry hair over a rock-hard abdomen, a shudder shimmied through her. As her hand moved lower just a bit, something thick and semi-hard nudged her fingers, wanting attention.

Without any real thought, she wrapped her hand around it. Soft, yet hard. Still, yet beginning to pulse within her grip. Half awake, she was intrigued. Trained to experiment, she moved her thumb up and down a protruding line. A vein? At her action, the whole length jerked, expanded in her grasp. Her fingers crept upward again, and she thumbed across the tip, making the man tremble. Making him give a quiet moan.

Her heart raced, thumping hard against her chest. Reality slipped closer and teased at her budding consciousness.

"Hmmm, that's real nice," a familiar deep voice growled. A large hand covered hers and gently squeezed. "Best wake-up enticement ever."

For a second, the words didn't make sense. She had been dreaming, right? Experimenting in her lab. Even though what she played with seemed not right in her work place.

"Oh, Lord!" Essie's eyes flashed open. Her gaze shot to where her hand lay. *What* it touched. "I-I-I...." *When* did she crawl onto the sofa bed with Trevon? *Why?* Sometime in the wee hours, she must have lost all her good sense.

She stared at her hand, at his thick shaft. *Let go of it!*

Her traitorous fingers didn't uncurl. And his hand held hers in place. Not with force, but enough she couldn't just pull it away. Truthfully, she didn't want to. This was ...so wicked, so naughty. She had never acted this way with any other man, and only a few times with Trevon. Even then, she'd been timid about it. She liked this new brazen side of her.

In the daylight slipping through the partially open Cape Cod-style shutters on the sliding glass doors, she noticed his blue eyes were almost navy as he stared at her. Amusement danced in their depths. "I guess we've moved beyond those first meeting again jitters."

She studied the stubble on his square jaw, found it as appealing as ever. The dimple at the side of his mouth still fascinated her, too. There was a whole lot to enjoy about the six-foot-three, naked man she clung to like plastic wrap. She should un-cling herself. They weren't ready for this step yet. Right? Well....

He chuckled, the rumbling sound making his chest rise and fall oh so nicely. The thick erection in her grasp grew even more, pulsed. "It's been a long time since you...uh...examined me so thoroughly." His sexy mouth so sinful and tempting grinned at her. "Ever the curious one, aren't you, sweetheart?" His dimple deepened. "I'm not complaining."

His teasing got to her, and she released him, which he allowed. "Sorry." Her face heated, and she frowned in confusion. "I have no idea how or when I ended up here." She forced her gaze to stay on his face, instead of drifting lower again. "Or why." *Lie.* The *why* was because she wanted him, no matter the problems of their past.

Heat flared in his eyes, like the spark in a fire taking hold. He gave her a gentle smile. "Exhaustion must have kept me from noticing you joining me here. Maybe those few drinks helped, too." He reached over to stroke the side of her face, causing her cheek to tingle, an ache building inside her going all the way down to her toes. "I sure don't mind. As I guess you've noticed."

She had, and that was one of their many problems. Okay, she couldn't control her gaze any longer. It slid down and found his cock appearing even longer, thicker. Had he been so large back in their day? How could she have forgotten? Would *that* possibly fit inside her? She worried her lower lip.

"It'll fit just fine," he said with gritty promise. "It always did."

She dropped her head to his chest, mortified. "I

said that out loud?"

"I'm pretty sure you didn't mean to, but, yes." He trailed fingers ever so softly up and down her back, making her shiver all over. "Since we've gotten past the undressing part—"

She groaned. "I've become a slut," she mumbled against his chest, unable to look at him. She had gone past being bold to fondling a man without his permission. And she was certain she'd worn her new nightie to bed. What had happened to it? Was she now sleep undressing? Sleepwalking?

"I'm embarrassed." They knew each other's bodies well, but they hadn't been like this together in a long time. Besides, weren't they going to take things slow? Although, she did remember telling him she didn't want to wait too long...for whatever they were going to do. Sex, she hoped. Definitely sex.

His long fingers moved lower, dipping to trail along her butt crack. She stiffened, pulled in a breath, and then shivered even more. Every cell in her body knew something was coming, something wonderful.

"First, you're *not* a slut." He lightly spanked one bottom cheek and snagged her attention. "Don't ever think that again."

Startled and more than a little excited at the light tap to her bottom, she blinked up at him. "And?" she prodded, curious about what else he would tell her. Warmth curled inside her, everywhere.

He went back to gliding his fingers over her quivering buttocks. "And I think you're a woman with powerful needs, more so than in the past. Which captivates me." He slipped a finger to her crease, slid it lower, then lower, and stopped.

Her entire body felt tight, enjoying sensations

she hadn't experienced since being with him. It screamed in protest. She felt cheated. Annoyed, she frowned at him. "Why did you stop?"

One corner of his mouth quirked up, and devilment shone in his eyes. "Because I think we should take this to the real bed."

Fine with her, but maybe she should insist on going slower—ignore that she'd already slid naked into bed with him. Didn't she want to talk to him about what went wrong between them before? Even if she fought with every breath the desire to just jump his bones, or have him jump hers.

"Such deep thoughts, Essie," he said, huskiness echoing in his voice, desire. "Trust me. Give me a chance."

She'd come here for reasons that were fading in importance in her mind. She'd been wrong, anyway. They hadn't even been together a full day yet, certainly nothing about her heart was involved. She'd admitted to him about approaching the matchmaker because she wanted to let her inner wild woman out, to be with a sexy beast of a man to give her one special night to remember forever. He'd shared about his request for a chance to bring out his seductive side that had gotten lost along the way in his current relationships. Surely, they could satisfy both of their goals. Besides, she was more than interested in experiencing his "seductive side," which she hadn't seen much of in the past.

"So, you're willing to compromise on why you sought out Madame Evangeline's help? Showing a romantic side instead of only your aggressive sexual side?" She glanced back at him. "To at least partially meet my request for a man to show exactly that...his sexy beast, his aggressive sexual nature."

"Can't we both compromise on our goals? I'll give you a taste of the intensity you think you want. And you'll accept my efforts to seduce you."

Not a bad compromise, from her point of view.

She pushed his arm away and shifted around to sit up beside him. "I would be getting pretty much a win-win."

"So would I." He looked with determination at her.

She should be rational, instead of letting her needs be in control. "Maybe we should leave our situation alone. We went our separate ways already, and maybe we should keep on that path." She sensed going their separate ways this time would be harder. She shouldn't have agreed to this arrangement.

His brow furrowed, but she decided to offer him a way out of making things between them more complicated. "We could just spend some friendly time together here. Go sightseeing." Not really her preference. "Go see the famous Grand Canyon of the Pacific, Waimea Canyon."

He sat up, shaking his head, looking at her with a lot of heat. A very firm erection stood out like a flagpole in front of him. He gripped it and grinned as she struggled not to stare. "No. We are *not* playing tourist, which I don't think you really want to do."

"But—"

"Do you recall my hand slapping your bottom in teasing? It could spank your sweet ass for real if you don't stop being so stubborn." He stroked his length, holding her gaze. "You were always stubborn; that much about you hasn't changed."

She gulped, and her buttocks clenched, a heat

building inside her. He kidded her, right? Still, the wicked concept teased her mind. Could he tell his threat stimulated her? She blushed, remained silent, but couldn't stop watching him, fascinated by what he was doing.

Another long, slow stroke. "The only 'sight' I'm interested in 'seeing' is you, Essie. Stretched out over a nice big bed. Spread open for me to feast on."

Her eyes widened, and she pulled in a shivery breath. She worried her pounding heart would cause a heart attack or something. Her clit throbbed, begging to be touched. Not to be outdone, her labia quivered, making her anxious with a more powerful ache than she had ever experienced. "That sounds...." She couldn't put a word to it.

He smirked, amused. "You want it, don't you, sweetheart? You really do." His gaze moved over her, settling on her breasts, with clear appreciation.

He'd always been good to them. Both areolas hardened. The breasts felt heavy.

"No, I don't!" she lied for some insane reason and then stood to pad back into the bedroom.

Surprising her, he scooped her up halfway inside the room. She squealed and struggled for about a millisecond. Being picked up like this by a strong man was exhilarating. But she wouldn't admit it to him.

"Put me down." Did the protest sound as feeble as she thought? More like "*never* put me down."

Two strides later, he did. He dropped her right in the middle of the rumpled bed. "Better?"

Before she could respond, he followed her down, pinning her to the mattress with his well-toned body. He squished her for a couple of breaths, which she didn't mind. And then he pushed up on muscled arms to look down at her, his sexy-and-I-know-it expression in place.

"This is wrong." If she had a few minutes, she could come up with a list of reasons. Until then she didn't hate it. In truth, she'd never been so aroused. Everything inside her pulsed, tingled, cried for more.

His erection pressed against her stomach, reached all the way up to her belly button. His soft, smooth balls rubbed her mound, ground ever so carefully, and more waves of incredible sensations swept over her.

"How is this wrong?" his question came out breathily.

Wrong? What? Oh, yes. "Because...." She couldn't come up with a good answer. Her brain cells were in a state of confusion.

He leaned down. His blue eyes focused on her. Intense, goal-minded. Here it was! He would kiss the daylights out of her. *Yes, yes, yes!* Instead, his lips met hers with a gentleness that surprised her. It pleased her more than if he had crushed his mouth to hers. He didn't even open his mouth, but the experience sent spirals of fire through her. A delicious burn.

Too soon, he lifted his head. He kept it close enough for her to feel his hot breaths, inhale his musky scent combined with some lingering smell of his familiar woodsy aftershave.

"More," she begged after a second. "Please."

"As you wish." Again, their mouths met, not in a rush, not in a demand. Simply learning one another again. Drawing pleasure from the simple act.

She reached up to circle his neck with her hands,

liked the immediate tension in his shoulders before he relaxed. As if he understood she was ready for the next step, he tilted his head to the side, becoming more intense with kissing her. She closed her eyes. *More, more, more! Don't ever stop.*

His tongue brushed against her lips, which tickled at the touch. The delicious sensation spread all the way down to her toes again. Even they tingled.

Eager for still more, she opened her mouth enough to let his seeking tongue slip inside. For just a second, their tongues met, and she trembled as the tips teased one another. He trembled, too—she suspected from the effort of holding back, because she felt tenseness thrumming through him.

Too many years had been wasted being cautious. She hauled Trevon closer and gave in to his expertise with French kissing. She moaned. *Oh, God she'd missed this.*

So lost in the moment, it took Trevon a few seconds to realize the bells ringing weren't from inside his head, pealing out his pleasure. No, the offending sound came from his cellphone in the other room. Why hadn't his voice mail kicked in? Damn phone!

Essie stiffened beneath him, nearly biting his tongue as she closed her mouth in annoyance. She pushed his shoulders back, her pretty face pinched in displeasure. "Seriously? You couldn't stop your calls even for a day or so?"

He sat on his haunches and glowered. "I thought I told everyone not to call me."

She huffed, and those magnificent breasts he so

wanted to play with rose and fell with her irritation. "Talk about a mood spoiler." Her pinched expression made it clear she remembered other times when he'd put business before her.

The darn phone kept right on ringing. He wanted to crush it beneath his foot. She was right; the call brought a rapid ending to what had promised to be a spectacular beginning. He'd lost ground with her already.

Frustrated beyond words, he climbed off the bed to stalk toward the offensive phone. He snatched it up and barked, "Trevon!"

"Is that any way to answer the phone, son?" his father snapped in response.

Trevon sucked in a calming breath. The one person he hadn't told about his going away for the weekend, of course. They didn't talk every day, so he hadn't thought about letting either his father or his brother know.

"Dad, this isn't a good time." Not at all.

"Another hot date?" His father heaved a disgusted sigh. "We need to talk. ASAP. Here. Kiss her good-bye, send her home or whatever, and get in your car. You can be here by this evening."

Trevon sank down onto the sofa bed, and Essie's light, feminine scent drifted up to him, souring his mood. Time ticked by faster with every passing minute. This wasn't the reserved little chemist from before. She was bolder, more determined, daring. Daring enough to have made an arrangement with a matchmaker to meet a man who would give her some seriously hot memories. Thank the Fates, he had been given the opportunity to be that man. He didn't intend to blow this second chance with her

"Not going to happen, Dad." He glanced toward the other room, relieved Essie hadn't left the bed. She might be pissed at him, but she waited for him. The idea perked his depressed shaft back to life.

"Sam and I—"

"I'm not even in Texas right now." He caught Essie's attention, and their gazes locked. He gave her a hopeful smile and held up a finger to signal he wouldn't be long. "And I won't be back until late Monday afternoon."

"What the hell? Where are you?"

Tired of the conversation not going anywhere, Trevon stood and went to his travel kit on the bathroom counter. Locating the condoms he had brought along interested him far more than whatever his father wanted to say.

He found the box, started to pull one out, but then grabbed the whole thing. Better to put it closer to the bed, be prepared. "In Kauai."

"With some woman?" his father accused, sounding disheartened.

"Dad, we are *not* having a discussion about your disapproval of my lifestyle. Not now. Not ever again if I can avoid it." He headed back to the bedroom. "I know I'm a huge disappointment to you. You want me settled down, giving you grandchildren. It is not going to happen. Accept that."

His father took a second before he said, "I just want you happy, and I don't think you are."

Essie looked at him with an uncomfortable expression and pulled the sheet over her. *Damn.* What had she heard to upset her? His comment about not wanting to settle down? A hint of hope came to life inside him. But did he really want it ? A

63

future with her? He'd wanted to make up for hurting her in the past by not trying to stop her from leaving, to see if there could be anything real between them this time. She had been on his mind for a while. Why the hell hadn't he called her? Was his ego that big?

This conversation got in the way. "Since you didn't say this was an emergency, Dad, I'll talk to you when I get home." At his father's reluctant grunt of agreement, he disconnected and tossed the phone on the bedside table. Then he picked it up again and turned it off.

He stood next to the bed, holding the box of condoms. "Any chance we can get back to where we were before the interruption?"

It took longer for Essie to answer than he would have liked, but she gave an uncertain nod. "I suppose."

Her gaze shifted to his cock, which—thankfully—decided to try its own method of tempting her by swelling again. Some of her uncertainty faded.

"I promise to make it up to you." Suddenly, giving this woman everything she wanted was important to him. He could be a "sexy beast." And he would make sure she learned just how romantic he could be and how much she could enjoy the experience. After thinking about their short year together, he realized he hadn't done much to show her that side of him.

She studied him in silence, watched him pull out a condom and toss the box on the small table. As he ripped the package open with his teeth and then grabbed his cock to roll it on, she drew in a soft breath. Her small tongue slid over her lower lip. The action enticed him to move faster.

He reached for the sheet, and she let him. Relief joined with his urgent need to move this along. In an instant, he climbed onto the end of the bed, stopping next to her slender feet with their painted toenails. For some reason, they captured his attention, and he smoothed his hands along the sides of each one. Silky soft.

She inhaled sharply, and her long legs stilled. When he picked up one foot and lifted it toward his mouth, she gasped.

"What are you doing? Have you developed some kind of foot fetish?" She gulped, but she didn't jerk her foot away.

Grinning at the idea, he kissed the top of her foot, stroked the bottom with his other hand, earning a squeal. "Still ticklish?"

This time, she did pull her foot away. "Yes." But she didn't look upset with him anymore. More curious about what he might do next.

The temptation to pick up her foot again was strong, but the desire to do far more was stronger. He noticed the moisture beaded on the curly hair of her muff. His pulse raced in his veins, and his brain shifted into a higher gear. He wanted to plunge into her warmth, drive deep, and take her fast and hard. The "beast" in him ready to be let loose.

Fighting for control, he met her gaze. "Whatever you want, honey. Name it. I'll do it." Or he would try damn hard to do anything she desired.

"Really?" she asked, sounding hopeful.

"Anything but stopping now." He would die if he couldn't have her, soon.

Those expressive eyes turned smoky warm. Her breath hitched, and the smile she gave him did him in. He wanted to spread those long, shapely legs wide and slide into her as deep and hard as she could handle. He ached for it so much he almost shook with the need.

When he took too long, she furrowed her brow. "What are you waiting for? An invitation?" She pulled her legs up and shifted her thighs apart, presenting him with a precious sight that stopped his breath. "Something like this?"

She kept surprising him. Bold and determined. *God, I love this change in her.*

"The offer is only good for so long. My legs are already getting tired of this position." Yet she continued to stay open to him.

He groaned at her brazenness, and his cock swelled even more. "I love a pushy woman."

"It's something new I'm trying out."

"Well, I like it."

Trevon inched forward, bent over to touch her center, wet with arousal. His gut tightened, sensing trouble. You would think he was a newbie at this. *Damn.* "I'm not sure how long I'm going to last this time," he grumbled in annoyance.

She gave him a confused look. Distracting her, he thrust one finger past her soft lips, deep into her heat. Tight. The realization gave him a real rush. "Oh, honey," he groaned again, pulled his hand almost away, and slid two fingers back inside her moist body.

"Oooh," she gasped, clenching around him. She smiled at him like a temptress and squeezed her inner muscles around his fingers. "Well, we've got most of today. Tomorrow, too, if you want." She arched her lower body upward, still clamping onto his fingers. "And you've got a whole box of condoms that shouldn't go to waste."

Blood pumped faster all through him, pooling at his intense erection. "They won't." He had a goal: use every one of the rubbers. It wouldn't be a problem.

He looked longingly at her breasts. He had been thinking about them ever since seeing her in the low-cut, kill-a-man dress. But he didn't think he could take the time to play with them right now. Much longer and he would explode without even sliding his cock inside her, which would be humiliating.

As if she read his mind, she cupped those luscious, fleshy mounds and flitted her thumbs over the nipples, teasing him as they budded. "Later. You can pay homage to these later."

He groaned. "You're not playing fair."

Chapter Six

Essie held Trevon's fascinated gaze and went from playing with her nipples to massaging her breasts. His eyes turned even darker. She experienced an aching longing more powerful than ever before. She had "played fair" too much in the past with Trevon. He'd seemed more interested in pleasing himself than her, and she'd gone along with it, afraid to ask for more. Her needs were handled in private. Stupidly.

To be fair, Trevon had taken his time with her when they'd first become intimate. But all too soon their lovemaking became hurried. His personal life and his business life demanded the bulk of his time. So, she'd ended their relationship. Now, he wanted another chance with her, as much as she did with him.

"God, Essie," he moaned again, continuing to watch her play with her breasts. His fingers were inside her, wiggling ever so slightly in his distraction.

But she felt them, and the delightful sensations grew stronger. "Ohhh, that feels so good!" Much better than when she pleasured herself. Giving over to the wonder, she dropped her hands to her sides.

Those wonderful digits moved again, and his thumb slid along her tingling labia, teasing her sensitive nub. Her hips jerked upward. Her head buzzed. No, it was happening all over her. "Again," she commanded, desperate.

Trevon kindly obeyed, and she wanted to bless him, even as she fought down another wave of quivering. "You used to do this," she gushed, barely able to focus on him. "Until you stopped...taking the time."

He worked her some more, his expression filled with regret. "I'm sorry. I can't say any more."

She shuddered, clamping around his fingers, aching, growing frantic. Her heart hammered. "Don't fail me this time," she implored. "Don't!"

His face tightened with strain, and the fingers moved faster, his thumb rubbing her hardened clit faster as well. "Come , sweetheart," he grunted. "Because I can't wait much longer to drive inside you."

Her thoughts were scattering. She gave over to what he was doing, to what her body required. She squirmed, panted, bucked against his hand. It didn't take long before she stiffened then rode out her orgasmic climax in a frenzy. "Trevon. Oh, Trevon!"

As she lie limp and recovering, she studied him through a haze of incredible satisfaction. Had she ever experienced anything like this? No. Again, she felt cheated. She wouldn't be settling for anything less than this in the future—whoever she ended up with.

She trembled as his fingers eased from her and noted the moisture coating them. He sat back and smoothed it around his condom-covered penis. His testicles appeared larger. His jaw rigid; his eyes heated. Ready for her. Her sated body came to life again. Ready for him.

"Your turn," she encouraged.

"This will be for *both* of us," he insisted. His eyes were so dark she couldn't tell they were blue anymore. His nostrils flared more with each deep inhale.

Yeah! But she didn't say it out loud, just waited in eager anticipation. Round two of him getting back in her good graces.

He moved closer between her legs and put a hand on each inner thigh, holding them apart. The mere touch made her suck in air, tense. His gaze locked with hers, determined, in control. She loved his reaction.

"Ready?" The question came out in a deep, breathy growl. "Because I'm going to fuck you now."

He had never spoken to her that way before. His crudity both surprised and pleased her, as did the promise in his gaze, the heat sparking between them. Suddenly, she wanted this to be different than any other time, when everything had been so...well, so basic and boring. The times when she lay on her back and he'd been on top of her. Not awful, just...ho-hum. She didn't want to be the same sexual wallflower. It was time those lessons in assertion paid off.

"Page ninety-five," she commanded. Her mind seeing a sexual position from the last manual she had read.

"What?" he asked in strained confusion.

As he started to guide his thick rod to her lower lips, she called out, "Wait!"

He froze, frowning, breathing hard. "Changed your mind? Please, no."

She shook her head. "Well, sort of." She jutted her chin out. "From behind," she proposed. "Doggy style."

One thick eyebrow lifted in curiosity. "Are you sure?" Waiting looked hard for him, his face red, his chest muscles taut.

"Definitely." Maybe she would hate it, but she wanted to try it.

Trevon gave a curt nod then moved back.

Yes! Essie scrambled around until she knelt on all fours in front of him, just like in the book. Kneeling here with her bare ass facing him seemed so naughty. "Is this right?" she asked, pretty confident.

"Let's change it a bit." He moved behind her, nudged her legs apart, and gently pushed her head to the mattress. "You'll like this better. Trust me."

"Page ninety-seven," she muttered, remembering this position, too. It should make the woman feel more sensations. She was all for that.

"What is with the page thing?" He gripped her hips with his strong hands.

Her face heated. "Um, a book I looked at," she admitted in a whisper.

"Ah, about sexual positions," he said, with a hint of tense amusement. He pulled her butt cheeks apart and put the head of his cock to her anus. "If you want to try them all, I'm game. Did you bring the book?"

Yes, but she would have to think about showing it to him. *Think later.* Wanting to get him focused again, she pushed her bottom back, like she'd also read about. The swollen head slid just inside her, and she shivered in anticipation. "I thought you were in a hurry," she challenged, impatient for the whole experience.

"Guess you are, too." In the next breath, he drove his shaft deep in one long thrust and held still.

"Ohhh!" she gritted out, holding her breath as she adjusted to the sudden fullness within her. It didn't hurt, but, oh wow!

He waited patiently, without speaking, without moving, but she suspected suffering.

Finally, she said, "I'm all right." She glanced back at him. Yes, suffering, if the tightness in his expression and deep breathing were signs. "Are you okay?"

He nodded, clenched his jaw tighter. He watched her for another second, making certain he believed her.

The sight of such a powerfully built man kneeling behind her, his long cock buried to the hilt, holding her in place, made her tremble. It was so much better than anything mentioned in the books. Something she would remember forever.

With a relieved look, he started moving in and out, slowly. She watched, fascinated by the experience. Intrigued by the way his facial expressions changed from determination to desperation to almost pain. Feeling her own changes growing, she turned her head and gave in to just enjoying everything he did. He fucked her hard, as he'd vowed he would. His balls slapped against her with every thrust.

Heat flared within her. Tension gripped her. She struggled to breathe, heard his ragged breaths. Once more, she readied for something amazing, a second orgasm.

She grunted with the intensity of the thrusts. "Oh, God."

"Give in. Now," he ordered and slammed into her with another brutal piston that forced her head harder against the mattress.

Essie screamed as another explosion ripped through her. She held still, pulse thrumming all through her as it rocked her. She felt weak, lightheaded, and would have collapsed to the bed if he hadn't held her up.

But he kept her in position, not finished yet. Thrust after thrust, shoving her forward. His panting grew louder, longer until he drove deep a final time and roared out his climax. "Oh, Essie! Damn, Essie!"

He collapsed over her back for a few seconds, still inside her but shrinking. She felt the sweat on his body and didn't care. She'd sweated, too.

It took another couple of minutes before he slid out of her and sucked in air. "Are you all right?"

She stretched out like a contented cat sleeping in the sun and turned to face him. "Better than all right. I'm boneless."

He grinned, pleased, as he steadied his breathing and eased down next to her. He nodded toward the box of condoms. "I hope I brought enough." He grinned even more. "Just how many positions have you read about? Want to try?"

She shifted onto her side, scooting against him, smiling sassily, encouraged by his attitude. "I think there were 365. And I'm fascinated by *all* of them."

He groaned, but amusement simmered in his blue gaze. "We'll need more condoms."

Toying with his smattering of chest hair, she smiled. "I think they have a small store here at the resort."

***

Trevon's eyes blinked open, and he took in the darkened bedroom, the lingering musky scent of their lovemaking. He should be exhausted. Instead, he felt revved up, energized. Maybe not ready yet for another round of heart-pounding, test-his-stamina sex, though.

He heard light snoring beside him and smiled. He doubted Essie would own up to being a snorer. He found it adorable.

Shifting, he glanced at her, dead to the world. Mr. Sexy Beast—he rather liked the name now—had more than done his job. They had used up most of those condoms. He felt darn good. She was an amazing lover, eager to try anything and everything, probably the scientist in her. And limber, oh man. He still couldn't believe how keen she'd been to try the crazy "Indian Headstand" thing in her book. More like she acted as a wheelbarrow, braced on her arms, him holding her up, legs wrapped around his back. He'd studied the pictures to get it right. And what about that "Dolphin" thing? With her braced on her neck, torso lifted and arched upward, her legs behind him. More study time on his part. He couldn't let her down.

His pulse raced. He started to sweat, again. *Whew!* And she'd stroked his ego with compliments more than a few times. A definite surprise this time, wild. Had he missed the signs before? What an idiot he'd been. She was a hell of a woman, and she lit one fire after another inside him.

After a quick trip to the bathroom, he strolled naked toward the main room, quietly closing the bedroom door behind him. The digital clock on the DVR told him it was in the wee hours of the morning. Their last day together. The idea bothered him, a lot.

He went to the sliding doors and moved the triple panel of shutters to one side so he could look out over the beach. The pitch-black sky held a handful of twinkling stars far, far away. The light from a full moon sparkled on the rolling waves. He liked it here.

He smiled, remembering their mid-afternoon drive into Lihu´e and farther up the coast to Wailua. They had needed a break. Okay, *he* needed a break. He wasn't as young as he used to be. His endurance wasn't as robust these days. She'd teased him a bit about it. He smiled again. She'd never teased him in the past. He liked this playful, demanding side of her.

His "break" had been to a change of locations for some extremely hot, quickie sessions. Near Wailua Falls then around Opaeka´a Falls. Oh, yes, seriously nice.

The phrase "You're not in Texas anymore," passed through his thoughts. When he told Essie about considering buying a place in Maui, he'd only been playing with the idea. He did want to do it, but here on Kauai instead. Because of their time together here, how she had made him enjoy everything about the island. This would be a great place to get away from the stress of his business and everything else. Maybe she would come with him sometimes. He would have to discuss the possibility with her.

Essie Reynolds possessed an interesting sense of humor, an amazing mind, and an enjoyment of challenges. The engineer in her. He regretted taking her for granted in the past. He remembered her being inquisitive before, but she was far more so now, about everything. Especially sex. Dear Lord, she was curious about that. Which made him an extremely lucky man. For the moment. Soon, they would go back to their real lives.

The idea saddened him. He'd wanted a second chance with her, and so far they were getting along well. But had he made up for failing her in the past? He still didn't know.

His cock grew hard thinking about Essie in the other room. After their weekend together, he would need some serious recovery time.

Tired and sore, Essie lay flat on her back, feeling aches everywhere. For a second, she couldn't understand why. Then her face heated, and she knew exactly why she felt this way. She had done some things that would challenge a contortionist...with Trevon. *Oh, Lord!* Her inner wild woman had definitely burst free. Kendra would be proud of her. But Essie.... Well, she wasn't sure how she felt, other than sore.

The smell of coffee drifted into the room, and she inhaled deeply. Her lifeblood.

"Daylight's wasting, as they said in the old Westerns." Trevon walked to her side of the bed and sat down. She glanced with caution at him. He smiled, setting a cup of coffee for her on the bedside table. "Good morning."

His rumbly voice caused warmth to curl through her. He had cleaned up, shaved, and already dressed in jeans without a shirt. She missed his sexy shadowed beard but liked the impressive bare chest. She remembered threading her fingers through the smattering of hair there, nibbling on his nipples. And more.... A lot more.

"How long have you been up?" She struggled to meet his eyes, a little shy. She scooted back and leaned against the headboard, pulling the sheet over her breasts. She winced, hoping he didn't notice. "Why didn't you wake me earlier?"

The man missed nothing, at least it seemed so this time. "I was restless, so I got up a while ago." He reached to smooth the bangs out of her eyes, his fingers whispering against her forehead and sending a shiver through her. "I let you sleep because you needed it. A bit sore, aren't you? Sorry."

Essie tried to ignore her blushing, ridiculous after what they had done together. She held onto the sheet with one hand and reached for the coffee with the other one. "You're my hero." She took a sip, sighed. "It's wonderful."

"You're good for my ego. Praising my abilities, including making a simple cup of coffee." He eased back, focusing on the sheet she gripped. "I've already seen every inch of your delicious body, sweetheart. I'm hoping to see it all again. Soon."

She liked his casual attitude, his light teasing, the assurance in his voice and in his heated eyes. He was good for her, too. Really good. He had done everything she'd wanted to try. Not once did he make her feel crazy for being pretty much a sex-crazed woman. So, why did she hide her body from him?

As she released the sheet and it fell to her waist, he drew in a breath, nostrils flaring. Pleasure filled her. "So what's the plan for today, lover boy?"

His gaze darted to the box of condoms on the other nightstand. "See how many more of those we can use up."

"You're not too...." She didn't want to say "tired" or "worn out" and wound his male pride. But they had gone at it hard, aggressively...a lot.

He chuckled. "It's been a long time since I worked out that hard. But I'm game."

She focused on the bulge in his jeans and smiled. "Glad to hear it." Her stomach rumbled and she groaned. "Sorry."

"How about we go grab some breakfast? After you shower." He stood, grinned, and waggled an eyebrow. "Want to shower together, save water?"

They had done that twice the day before, neither time being quick. He really liked to play with the soap. Why hadn't they done it in their past? She had so many regrets, and she couldn't place all of the blame on him.

"Maybe later. I'm in more of a hurry this time. I'm starving." If she remembered right, they hadn't eaten since stopping in a little diner in Wailua.

He shed his jeans, and she discovered she wasn't as hungry as she'd thought. At least not for food. As she climbed out of bed and into his embrace, her heart raced, even as dread began filling her. Their last day together. They would return to their own, very different lives. Unless....

"Don't think about leaving right now," he said gently. He cupped her buttocks and pressed her against his thick erection. "Just give us both this one final day to indulge ourselves, fulfill our desires." He smiled down at her. "To try out some more of those

365 positions."

She blinked back sudden tears and forced a lightness to her tone she didn't feel. "To finish that box of condoms."

Chapter Seven

"Oh, Kendra, what am I going to do?" Essie sat behind her desk two weeks later. Nothing in her life seemed right. She couldn't get her head into the project she was supposed to be leading. She avoided talking to any of her family. And she'd let her friend's phone calls go to voice mail until today.

"About?" Kendra prodded. She hesitated and asked, "I'm worried about you. Do you want me to come see you? My guys will take care of Evie. I can—"

"I adore you for wanting to drop everything and come here to be with your poor, pitiful-me friend. But I'll get through this." Being this depressed was ridiculous. Trevon had given her everything she requested from their one-night stand, and much more.

Kendra sighed on the other end of the line. "I should never have gotten you mixed up with Madame Evangeline. I just thought…. Well, it worked out so great for me. Shane, Carson, and Evie are my life."

Sniffing back a tear of envy, Essie looked at the brochure from the resort. It was nearly worn out by her looking through it over and over and over. She hadn't looked at the many photos she and Trevon had taken. Maybe someday. Not yet. Her heart hurt too much with missing the incredible man. The man who hadn't called her since their return to Houston.

"I had an amazing experience. I can't complain about a second of it." A big, fat tear plopped onto the brochure and she dabbed it away. "I'm just being silly."

"He hasn't gotten in touch with you, has he?"

Essie heard the irritation in Kendra's voice. If she didn't take control of the situation, her friend would show her mother hen side, treat her like her chick that needed protecting. She felt the tiniest bit better. But she needed to deal with this on her own.

"No." She thought back to the original arrangements each of them made with the matchmaker. "He more than met what I requested. Way more." Trevon had earned another chance with her. Yet they hadn't talked about it before they left each other in the airport. Partly because he'd been on his phone with his partner from the second the plane landed.

She dashed at another tear. Maybe showing her new aggressive side had been too much for him. But unleashing her curiosity and his not objecting to trying whatever she wanted made her...well, uncontrollable. Everything had been such fun. That stupid book was the problem. She should never have bought it, never have become enthralled with all the possibilities. *What happened to that book? Whatever.* "I got too greedy," she mumbled.

"I doubt if he suffered," Kendra gritted out, annoyed. "You had sex, probably a lot of it, if I'm right. So the man *did not* suffer."

She couldn't deny the lots of sex part. "I'm just not sure what I did wrong."

Kendra snorted. "He's an idiot."

Essie jerked as someone knocked on her closed office door. Without even waiting for an answer, her father opened it and stepped into the room. He frowned. What had she forgotten this time?

"I've got to go, Kendra. My dad just came into my office. I'll call you later." Essie disconnected and slid the brochure under a stack of papers next to her monitor.

"What's the problem?" she asked, not quite meeting his eyes.

He walked closer. "You're back to dressing—"

"Don't go there, Dad." Some of her rebellious spirit had faded, more with each day since her return from Kauai. The change hadn't felt as important anymore.

"People are talking, Essie. They don't understand your mood lately." He blew out a breath, and she glanced up at him. "Your family is concerned about you." He took a second. "I'm worried."

His words almost made her tear up again. Showing emotion was a strain for him, so this caught her off guard. "I'll be fine," she said and gave him a weak smile. "I just have some things on my mind. Personal matters."

He shifted uneasily, still frowning. "This has to do with the little vacation you took a couple of weeks back, doesn't it? Did something happen? Something I...something I can help with?"

She blinked at sudden moisture in her eyes. "Nothing bad happened, Dad. But I appreciate your concern." There was nothing he could do, nothing anyone could do. Or *should* do. She just needed to get to the point where those incredible days were the memory she had wanted and not something she longed for.

"Your mother wants you to come to Sunday dinner this week." He looked uncomfortable. "She's missed you."

Essie smiled, her heart lightened. Her father had missed her being there, even when they disagreed on something. Maybe her mother as well, but *he* had come here and let her know his feelings, in his awkward way.

"I'll be there."

He breathed a sigh of relief, met her gaze, and said, "Maybe I'll ask Daniel, too. He has asked about you."

"No, Dad. Daniel needs to move on. I have." Now she needed to move on from thinking about Trevon Chanders every minute of every day.

Her father looked ready to protest but then nodded curtly. He turned toward the door. "Sunday, then. One o'clock."

After she watched him walk away, she glanced down at the simple dress she'd worn today. Comfortable, familiar, but it seemed wrong. She liked the jeans she'd worn before...before giving up on the new woman she wanted to be. The one she'd been while with Trevon.

She picked up the brochure, studied it with less pain than before, and put it in a drawer. He'd helped her take a big step forward in her life. Now she needed to manage the next ones on her own.

Her stomach tumbled with butterflies. She

should to tell her father she was quitting the company. She didn't know what she wanted to do next, but it wouldn't have anything to do with being a chemical engineer.

***

Trevon stretched out on his bed, tried to relax after so much happening in his world lately. But his thoughts wouldn't slow down. He'd returned from Kauai energized, body worn out, but mentally eager to make changes. Talking to Essie on the plane trip home helped. With her quick mind, she grasped the details, the possible problems, and then figured out how to make it work. He had never discussed his dream with the other women in his life. All they had ever been interested in was his body and how he could use it to satisfy them.

They were history. He'd ended each of the relationships his first week home. None of them cared. Sad as it should be, neither did he.

Essie, though, he missed. Sure, most of their time on the island had been all about sex. A whole lot of sex. Incredible times because she enjoyed it so much. She'd worked him damn hard, and he ached to do it all over again. He had earned another chance at a relationship with her, but he hadn't pursued it after leaving the resort. Why not? By now she would have put it all behind her and gone back to her normal lifestyle. The thought saddened him.

Put her aside. Let it go. There was so much more he had to focus on. His business partner was finally stepping up and taking over some of the PR work Trevon had always done. But he still needed guidance. At least Ed was fine with him easing away from so much heavy involvement with the firm. He'd even agreed to help with Trevon's starting the new company. To his relief, their discussion about it all had gone really well. Essie had told him to stop holding back, just move forward with the idea. He felt so much happier.

But what about her moving forward with her goals? She wanted to stop working for her father's oil company. She wasn't sure what she would do, but the job there no longer interested her. She admitted she didn't require the income. He wanted to know what was going on with her. Yet he hadn't tried to get in touch with her. Again, why the hell not?

His cell phone rang. *Essie!* Excitement curled through him before he tamped it down. Neither one had called the other. As he pulled the phone out of his slacks pocket, he read the caller ID. Dread wafted over him.

"Hello, Dad." He sat up, leaned against the headboard in the dimly lit bedroom.

"Your brother and I have been talking. We've decided to go in on that construction company with you."

Trevon blinked. Had he heard right? His father had been against the idea of the non-profit construction company to build homes for needy single mothers, believing it couldn't work. All they'd done was argue about it.

"I don't understand," he said cautiously. Also, they had never discussed his father and brother being involved with the new company. He wasn't opposed to the idea, just confused.

"Sam told me to stop being so stubborn. Stop

being determined to convince you to work for *our* company, something you have always been opposed to doing." His father drew in a breath. "He convinced me that your plan is a good one. And he wants to be part of it." He hesitated. "I do, too, son. If you'll let me."

Trevon tried to get a handle on the changes in his father's attitude. Sam wasn't a surprise, but his dad was. Slowly, he smiled. "Yes, I would love to have the two of you involved with this project." Another huge piece of the puzzle fell into place.

"Good, good." His father sounded relieved. "When can we get together in person and get the details figured out? Next week?"

Trevon almost jumped on the suggestion, but suddenly there was something else he wanted to do first. Someone he needed to talk to, to thank for giving him a verbal kick in the ass to get his plan out of his dreams and off the ground.

"The week after that. I'll call you about arrangements later." He took a second before adding, "Thanks, Dad."

He sat there for several minutes, stomach churning. Had he waited too long before contacting Essie? Should he just leave it all alone?

His gaze slid to the battered book on the dresser across the room. He'd found it as they were taking a final look around the condo for what they had brought with them. She either forgot it or didn't want it any longer. So he'd stuck it in his bag, along with the few unused condoms.

He latched onto his excuse to call her.

Her cell number was already back on his speed dial, although he'd never dialed it. Heart hammering, he placed a call.

When she answered, he warmed at hearing her voice. "It's Trevon. Have you got a minute?"

***

Standing at the resort's check-in counter, Essie couldn't believe all that had happened to her in the last forty-eight hours. She had given her notice at work, much to her father's frustration. She'd informed her mother she wouldn't be there this weekend for Sunday dinner. And she'd made last minute flight arrangements to Kauai. All because the sexiest man in the world had called her three nights ago. Finally.

She shifted, impatient, while the clerk finished her paperwork. Trevon's surprise call had made her fight hard not to break into tears. Just hearing his voice again turned her into a needy mess. She wanted to see him in person, wanted to touch him. She should have been more resistant to even talking to him. Especially when he asked her to meet him here. She hadn't even hesitated. How crazy was that?

Wrong man for her, right man. Who knew? Time would tell. And she wanted another chance to figure it out.

At Trevon's request, she wore the skintight white dress as before. She tingled, remembering how he vowed to strip it off her right away. In return, she insisted he wear those same worn jeans, which she would be stripping off him as well. This time, she only packed a small bag. She did learn quickly. And she hoped she'd overpacked again, even with this limited amount.

She battled the urge to scream at the clerk to work faster. Instead, she thought about Trevon some more. He promised to have a brand new box of condoms with him. She'd started to tell him that she would bring the infamous sex manual with her, but she remembered she hadn't been able to find it. But she thought they could wing it this time.

"Ms. Reynolds, I'll help you with your bag," the same teenaged boy as before said as he moved next to her. Then he blinked in sudden recognition. "Or is...?"

As she turned toward him, Trevon walked up and grinned at the boy. "I'll take it from here." He handed the teenager a large tip.

"You look...different," she said, studying him. "Less troubled?"

He ignored her bag and the few people nearby. He pulled her against him, his mouth claiming hers in the next breath, which he stole from her. If the size of the erection pressing at her was any indication, he'd missed her. Good. If he could read female signs, then he'd know by the way her hard nipples crushed into his chest and the way she quivered all over she'd missed him, too.

"Oh, sweetheart," he mumbled, releasing her the smallest amount. "We've got lots to talk about."

She wasn't interested in talking. She stretched up to whisper in his ear, "I'm not wearing any panties." She had taken them off at the airport, and it had felt wicked, naughty, too.

He grumbled, "You're killing me already." He eased her away and snagged her bag then took off in a near sprint toward the condo.

"Another race?" she teased, keeping up with him

eagerly.

He stopped to glance at her, a devilish look in his eyes. "Did we leave off with page 103 or...."

Her shoulders slumped. "I couldn't find the book."

He grinned, pleased. "Because I have it." He winked. "I've been studying up, too."

"You took my book?" Should she be upset with him? Nope. *Studying up?* That sounded promising. A thrill spiraled through her, ending low in her vagina. "My white knight."

"Hardly," he protested. "If I was one, I would have come after you much sooner than this." He held her gaze. "I took the book as my souvenir."

She laughed. Coming here was definitely the right decision. But she should act a little more mature, less lust-crazed. "So, what do we have to talk about?"

She thought back to their previous trip home, what they discussed on the flight. "You did it, didn't you? You decided to start the company." She was unbelievably excited for him.

He nodded, his blue gaze warm as he spoke. "Thanks to your encouragement. I stopped just thinking about the idea and put things in motion."

"More to celebrate," she said, happy for the first time in weeks.

They started walking, and he glanced at her, curious. "More?"

"I did it, Trevon. I quit my job." Uneasy at first, she felt at peace with the decision.

"Do you have some time for trying something new? Something well out of the chemical engineering field?" he asked, stopping again to look at her.

"Working with me?"

"That might be interesting." She thrummed with desire to get this handsome man naked and in bed. "How about we talk...later?"

"Probably for the best." His heated gaze swept over her, and he chuckled then reached to finger her short hair. "I can see in your eyes a serious conversation isn't on your mind right now." He stroked the side of her face with the back of his fingers. "But, later, I do want to discuss the possibility of your working with me."

The idea held a lot of appeal. She looked for a new challenge. "Okay." She leaned toward him, impatient. "Remember what I said in the lobby? The no panties thing?"

He groaned. "Page thirty-three, 'See-Saw.'"

She blinked. "Oh, I remember seeing that, too." She took his hand and dragged him down the sidewalk. "Come on, Sexy Beast. Time's a wasting."

About the Author

*Shoulda, woulda, coulda...*words from a song on the radio. Words that get right to a writer's heart, to her imagination. They certainly get to Starla Kaye's imagination. She's a full-time, bestselling writer and always observing life and the world around her, searching for new story ideas.

Starla has published eighty-six romance titles, including contemporary, historical Western, Regency, Medieval, paranormal, sci-fi, and GLBT. Her stories always lean toward the sensual side of romance, some even erotic. Whatever happens within her stories, the characters face difficulties between the outside world and each other. They always manage to find love and respect for one another.

The same has been true in Starla's life. She has faced many challenges. She long ago met and married a wonderful man who supports her in every way...just as she does him.

Other Books by Starla Kaye

Starting Over

The CEO and the Cowboy

Cowboy Dreamin'

Maggie's Secret Wish

Acceptance